Dear

Happy Birthday!! :-)

Best,
[signature]
107

Praise for A.P. Fuchs's *Axiom-man*™

"Axiom-man is that unique breed of superhero that seems almost lost amid today's gaggle of the dark and tormented. He's nice, he cares, and his strength comes not from his fantastic powers, but from his soul. A.P. Fuchs has written a defining superhero novel."
- Frank Dirscherl, author/creator of *The Wraith*

"Reading *Axiom-man* is refreshing, like reading about the early days of Peter Parker, but with a cooler villain as well."
- Jon Klement, author/creator of *Rush and the Grey Fox*

"*Axiom-man* was well worth reading and recommending. The broad appeal is amazing—from youth to adult, guys and girls. Superheroes might just become my thing."
- Susan Kirkland, reviewer, *Calhoun Times*

"Fuchs brings to life a wonderfully imaginative hero we can all relate to . . . . If you're looking for something different, something truly creative, yet filled with action, look no further. *Axiom-man* is the end of your search."
- David Brollier, author of *The 3rd Covenant*

"I found myself picking the book up at various points in the day, just to read a little more."
- Darryl Sloan, author of *Ulterior* and *Chion*

"If you're an action fan with moral sensibilities you'll not just enjoy *Axiom-man*, you'll wish you were he."
- Frank Creed, author of *Flashpoint*

"Plenty of surprising twists and turns in this highly enjoyable story. It'll leave you wanting more. Axiom-man is a delightfully human superhero with true depth and spirituality."
 - Grace Bridges, author of *Faith Awakened*

"If you dig superhero tales that are loaded with action and fun, look no further."
 - Nick Cato, *Horror Fiction Review*

"A must read that I cannot recommend enough."
 - Joe Kroeger, *Horror World*

THE AXIOM-MAN™ SAGA
BY A.P. FUCHS
(listed in reading order)

Axiom-man
Episode No. 0: First Night Out
Doorway of Darkness

ALSO BY A.P. FUCHS

FICTION

A Stranger Dead
A Red Dark Night
April (writing as Peter Fox)
Magic Man (deluxe chapbook)
The Way of the Fog (The Ark of Light Vol. 1)
Devil's Playground (written with Keith Gouveia)
On Hell's Wings (written with Keith Gouveia)

NON-FICTION

Book Marketing
for the Financially-challenged Author

POETRY

The Hand I've Been Dealt
Haunted Melodies and Other Dark Poems
Still About A Girl

Go to
www.apfuchs.com

EPISODE No. 0

AXIOM-MAN™
FIRST NIGHT OUT

by

A.P. FUCHS

COSCOM ENTERTAINMENT
WINNIPEG

Coscom Entertainment
Suite 16, 317 Edison Avenue
Winnipeg, MB R2G 0L9 Canada

This book is a work of fiction. Names, characters, places and events either are products of the author's imagination or are used fictitiously. Any resemblance to actual events or persons living or dead is purely coincidental.

ISBN 978-1-897217-71-9

Axiom-man and all other related characters are Trademark ™ and Copyright © 2007 by Adam P. Fuchs. All rights reserved.
Axiom-man Episode No. 0: First Night Out is Copyright © 2007 by Adam P. Fuchs. All rights reserved, including the right to reproduce in whole or in part in any form or medium.

Published by Coscom Entertainment
www.coscomentertainment.com
Text set in Garamond
Printed and bound in the USA
Cover pencils and inks by Justin Shauf
Cover colors by Kyle Zajac
Edited by Ryan C. Thomas
Interior author photo by Roxanne Fuchs

Library and Archives Canada Cataloguing in Publication

Fuchs, A. P. (Adam Peter), 1980-
      Axiom-man : episode #0 : first night out / A.P. Fuchs.

   ISBN 978-1-897217-71-9 (pbk.)

         I. Title.

PS8611.U34A944 2007   C813'.6   C2007-903382-2

To my sister, Kara, who taught me it's not who you were
that matters, but the value of who you are
after a new beginning.

EPISODE No. 0

AXIOM-MAN™
FIRST NIGHT OUT

PROLOGUE

GABRIEL GARRISON STOOD before his hallway mirror, shaking.

How did I—But he already knew the answer. This whole night had been a whirlwind, one that began with the blinding blue-white light of the messenger without a name.

Just moments before, he had returned home after . . . flying. After smashing mammoth wooden beams on a railcar into splinters. Things that human beings couldn't do. But those weren't the strangest happenings this night, as bizarre as they were. Upon returning home he had gone into the bathroom to rinse his hands and rid the skin of its dryness from the dirty beams. It was then he noticed himself in the mirror—the blue eyes, including pupils and whites—and the light blue sheen to his normally dark brown hair. Panicking, his vision lit up in bright blue, bathing his sight as though he were peering through a film of light blue cellophane. Soon the blue light gripping his eyes turned so bright he couldn't see a thing. Whether it was instinct or not, he reached up and touched his eyes, his fingers recoiling the moment they came in contact with crackling electric energy. The light grew brighter and more intense. Heart galloping inside his chest, he reached up to touch his eyes again, this second touch more painful than the first. He could only imagine the scorch marks on his fingertips. The light grew brighter and brighter, then—his eyes widened and a blast of brilliant blue power burst forth from his eyes, destroying the mirror in a loud, glassy crash.

He could see again, though the blue of his eyes remained.

Broken with fear, he remained cowering on the bathroom floor, trembling, eyes squeezed shut. His stomach flipped upside down with the notion that the strange blue energy might return and possibly burn the inside of his eyelids. Yet, at the same time, having this strange ability made perfect sense. He had been flying earlier, after all. He had somehow gained the strength of ten men combined, if not more. This latest—what did the messenger call it? Gift?—somehow made perfect sense. And if this was the last portion of this gift to manifest itself, so be it. He had already been given so much.

His eyes . . .

Gabriel shakily got to his feet and went to the hallway mirror and, sure enough, a different man than the one he was used to seeing stared back. A man with completely bright blue eyes and blue-sheened hair.

The same excited panic returned; the blue in his eyes grew brighter. Not wanting to blast the mirror to smithereens like he had the bathroom's, he widened his eyes like before and a small crackle of blue energy spewed forth, singeing the mirror, leaving a smudge in its wake, like someone had rubbed dark ash across the glass. Once more, he could see clearly, no blue light distorting his vision. But his hair was still blue. The mark of his powers?

Makes sense, he thought.

He wanted to study his visage, really examine himself, but he forced himself to look away, not wanting to accidentally trigger another blast of power. His heart beat fast; he fought the excitement building within, the same excitement that seemed to encourage these shots of energy from his eyes.

Breathing slow, rhythmic breaths, Gabriel pretended this night wasn't happening at all. No flying, no amazing feats of strength, no incredibly powerful energy spewing forth from his eyes. He was ordinary, nothing special. The messenger had not come. He was just Gabriel Garrison. Nobody and nothing more.

When he opened his eyes, he was relieved to see them dark brown again, the same with his hair.

It was over.

"Or is it over?" he whispered.

A part of him wanted it to be. A part of him just wanted it all to be a bad dream without repercussion. He had had trouble sleeping after all. And it was when he had checked his email earlier that the messenger appeared to him. A sleep-deprived hallucination, perhaps? No, it couldn't be. He'd had sleepless nights before and knew that, at least for himself, one night without sleep wouldn't be enough for him to start seeing and hearing things. More so, *doing* things, things only possible in a dream world and not here in reality.

And I know I did those things, he thought. *I remember it all clearly—the running, the leap into the air, partially lifting the jungle-gym—I did it all.* A smile came over his face. "I did it all."

Still shaking with adrenaline, he examined the mirror once more, the smudge-like black mark confirmation that none of this was in his head and everything had, in fact, happened.

Slowly, he turned from the mirror, then glanced back at the burn mark once more, as if this final double-check would cement in stone that he was no longer a mere human being but something more. What that *more* was, he didn't know. But it was different. *He* was different and not just because of the strange powers he now possessed. Something had shifted within and right now all he could attribute that feeling to was the fact he was no longer like everybody else.

With slow-moving legs, he went to the front room and gazed at the computer screen. It sat open to his email account; he hadn't closed it earlier when he'd torn off with a surge of energy and enthusiasm. But that's all it was. Just a regular computer screen void of the messenger's awesome presence.

Gabriel sat on the couch on the opposite end of the room and stared at the computer, partly expecting the messenger to show up again and further explain why he had given him these powers.

The minutes ticked by then quickly melted into an hour.

The messenger did not come.

More than anything Gabriel wanted to call up his folks and tell them what happened. Not that they could possibly provide any advice but tonight was the first *major* thing that'd happened to him since moving out on his own. He didn't know what to do or who, if anyone, to turn to. And he strongly doubted he *could* turn to anyone. Who could explain this to him? Who could offer him words of comfort and wisdom? Who else on the face of the earth had ever been granted abilities a person only dreamed about?

It was hopeless.

What if he was crazy? What if that black mark on the hallway mirror—even the shards of broken mirror in the bathroom—were somehow all an illusion, some screwed up mind game his brain was playing on him? He couldn't have anyone thinking he was crazy and he surely didn't want to think of himself as crazy either. If he went to a doctor to, what, have some tests done, what then? And what if it turned out to be true? What if something *was* there? Then what? Certainly he'd become the subject of endless tests and medical journals.

He put his face in his hands. "There's nothing I can do about this."

Tears leaked from the corners of his eyes. It wasn't long before the sobs grew deep and thick and he couldn't stop crying, his heart lost to the murk of loneliness and solitude.

"I don't know what . . . I don't know what to do . . ." His voice was thick and weak; he could barely even hear himself talk beneath the throat-wrenching cries. "I can't . . . I'm stuck . . . there's no . . ."

Why was this so hard? Earlier, when flying, the exhilaration made him feel like the most special and powerful man in the world. This sudden drop into despair—he didn't have an answer for that.

Thoughts of going to work shortly surfaced somewhere in the back of his mind. There was no way he'd be able to function. Worse, he didn't want to be a risk to anyone.

"Take this away from me," he said into the pool of tears in the palms of his hands. "I don't want this. Not right now. Not me. I don't care anymore."

He thought the messenger would somehow hear him and come and fix whatever it was the strange being of blue-light had started.

But Gabriel remained alone, sitting on the couch, his body bent over his thighs, face in his hands.

Only one thing was certain: he wasn't going anywhere today.

Chapter One

Sleeping had been useless.

Gabriel had tried to fall asleep shortly after calling work just after seven, leaving a message for his supervisor at Dolla-card, Rod Hunter, that he wasn't feeling well and would be using one of his sick days.

That's what they're there for, anyway, he had thought. *Might as well use them.*

Lying there in bed in his pajamas, mind reeling over all that happened earlier that morning—who could sleep? It wasn't long after his head hit the pillow that he began to feel that heart-quickening excitement that accompanied the surge of energy and vigor that came after receiving his powers. He tried his best to lie still and not think of anything, clear his mind of all thoughts and take slow, deep breaths in an effort to drift off to dreamland, but his body refused to relax.

Around eight, he got up, tired of trying to rest. When he stood from his bed, a swoon of dizziness came over him and he had to sit back down on the edge of the mattress. Fatigue made his head feel hollow and his limbs weak, but not in the same way he usually felt when deprived of sleep. He was tired, that was for sure, but there was a strong undercurrent of *drive* and *motivation* keeping him alert.

He rubbed his hands along the thighs of his gray-striped-blue pajama bottoms, ridding his palms of sweat. A lock of hair fell over his eyes and though the strands were so close to his eyes they were dark and blurry, he knew that his hair had turned blue again.

"Oh no," he breathed and pushed the hair out of his face. When his hand trailed a centimeter or so in front of his eyes, a tingling sensation skipped across his skin. And as if *feeling* that tingling were a trigger, blue light began invading his field of vision. "Not again. Not yet. Not till I can—"

The light grew brighter and brighter, flooding his sight so his bedroom closet across from his bed was bathed in pale blue. He squeezed his eyes shut, then clasped his hands over his eyes, like the lid of a pop bottle keeping the fizz from a Pepsi at bay. Even now, with his eyes shut, he didn't see the usual dark red of the inside of his eyelids but red overlaid with blue—a dark purple.

Panicking, his mind went blank as to what to do. The only thing he was aware of was the intense desire to avoid firing off another blast from his eyes and destroying the closet or floor.

Relax, he told himself. "Just breathe. How did I—" Memory of earlier that morning flooded back and he recalled how not thinking about his powers and thinking himself worthless somehow made the powers go away.

"You're nothing," he said. "You're a loser. A nobody. You're you before all this mess. Nothing more. Whatever you think is happening isn't happening at all. It's all in your head. Get rid of it. Shhhh . . . shhhh . . . shhhh . . ." He rocked back and forth a few times before resting his elbows on his thighs. *Just think of nothing. Nothing. Nothing.* Breathing slow and sure, he let his mind drift off till all he saw in his mind's eye was total blackness, the same darkness as his vision.

A flash of blue cracked before his vision, then utter darkness again.

Slowly, eyes still shut, he pulled his hands away from his eyes. Darkness. Just murky red.

"Slow, go slow," he said and opened his eyes just enough to see a blur of gray-striped-blue pajama pants at the bottom of his vision.

No blue energy leaked out.

Smiling, he opened his eyes all the way. A huge rush of relief filled his entire being when . . . nothing happened.

He took a deep, relieving breath and said, "Okay," on the exhale. "There. It's over."

He needed a plan.

———

Still wearing his pajamas, Gabriel sat cross-legged in the center of his front room. He glanced at the clock and was horrified to see it had been an hour since he had gotten up, which meant it took him the better part of an hour to come up with a plan for figuring this all out.

The idea hit him when, back in the bedroom, that excitement returned. It finally clicked and the realization that that excitement had something to do with his powers was like a breath of fresh air. It was an issue of—attitude?—he discovered, a mindset of some sort. Somehow thinking about his powers and what they enabled him to do was enough to draw them to the surface from wherever it was they went when he temporarily convinced himself he was only a regular human and nothing more. Something . . . shifted . . .

inside, as though a switch were activated, unleashing these powers into the forefront of his abilities.

The bedroom felt cramped so, deciding to use the only other big room in his apartment, he entered the front room, his mind focused entirely on him being nothing more than your average, everyday human being.

Now, sitting there, it was time to truly put his theory to the test and, more so, his plan on figuring these powers out. He had to know how to control these abilities, how to bring them forth then put them away. He wouldn't be able to function otherwise. And if he managed that, he'd get in front of the computer and call out to the messenger to come and explain himself and provide real instruction as to what these powers were for, or just take them away altogether.

Ready whenever you are, he told himself. *I'm not ready, but I'll do this.* Once more he yearned for someone to talk to and once more he was hit with the sickening slap to the heart that there wasn't anyone he *could* turn to. At least, not now.

"Oh, man, be careful," he whispered, and closed his eyes, removing the mental restraint that kept memories of the previous night locked away.

A quick mental flash of flying high over a field just outside the city was enough to get his insides excited. Suddenly, a flood of energy swept through him, saturating him through and through. It felt as if his bones had turned to iron. An alertness, the kind he only felt after a good night's rest, became his consciousness.

Slowly, he opened his eyes and was slightly disappointed to find his vision clear, without a hint of blue. He pulled a lock of hair down over his eyes . . .

. . . and grinned when he saw its blue highlights.

FIRST NIGHT OUT

Hands slightly shaking, he forced himself not to get too excited lest his eyes accidentally fill up with blue light and he disintegrate the couch across from him.

"Now do this backwards," he said and closed his eyes.

Like earlier, he bombarded himself with self-deprecating statements, some even derogatory—whatever it took to make himself believe he was no one special. As much as he hated it after a lifetime of feeling that way, he told himself he belonged on the bottom rung of the Ladder of Human Worth.

Blue light flashed before his eyes then vanished just as quickly as it came.

You're nothing, he thought.

He opened his eyes this time with a little more confidence and was thrilled when everything looked normal, his vision clear. He checked his hair.

It was dark brown.

———

One thing at a time. That would be the key to figuring this all out.

As much as Gabriel wanted to test out flying again, as deeply as his heart yearned to touch the sky once more, he forced himself to keep his feet planted. It was, after all, day time. If anybody saw him . . . . No, not yet. If ever. It was one thing to be able to do these things, another to determine *what* he was going to do with them once he knew what he was doing.

The next task was to learn about the tremendous strength he exhibited the night before. And the very thought of exploring that . . . talent . . . made him excited again. Instead of forcing himself to remain calm, he let the excitement fill him, let it take over. He checked his hair—blue.

The powers were on.

That's assuming that they need to be "on" in order for them all to work, he thought. That was a good question, actually. Did his powers need to be in "on" mode for all of them to manifest, or was the "on" mode only reserved for such special abilities like shooting blue energy beams from his eyes?

He calmed himself, this time with a little less effort than before. He checked his hair again: dark brown.

"Okay, what to lift," he said, scanning his front room. There wasn't anything here by way of weightlifting equipment or other traditional gauges of strength. Surely there had to be something he could use though. *Let's see: a couch, a chair, computer desk, TV, TV stand, pictures . . .* "Hmph, not much." Hands on hips, he took a deep breath. "Wait." He turned his attention to the couch, which was actually a hide-a-bed as opposed to your run-of-the-mill sofa. Getting that thing into the apartment took the work of him, his dad *and* his brother. The sucker weighed a ton.

"As good a thing to start with as any," he said and went over to where the couch met the wall.

With both hands, he gripped the corner, then pulled the couch a few inches from the wall so as to not damage the wall when or if things got crazy. He had to dig his heels into the carpet to even get the thing to move.

At least one thing's learned: gotta be in go-mode for me to even have a shot at lifting that thing on my own.

He rounded to the other side of the couch and, using the same maneuver, brought it further from the wall. He did the same thing a few times to either side, drawing the couch out further toward the center of the room until it was about four feet from the wall. That way, he figured, if he accidentally tipped the couch over either way, when it fell on its back or bottom it wouldn't hit anything and he'd be stuck using a part or all of his damage deposit to pay for the repair.

Gabriel took a deep breath then walked to the front of the couch. He didn't know much about lifting heavy objects other than that, according to his gym teacher, you were never to lift bending over and using your back. You were supposed to use your legs as much a possible if you had to lift something very heavy.

He squatted down and positioned his feet firmly beneath him. Placing his palms underneath the bottom edge of the couch, he focused on his powers, imagining himself doing what it was he was about to attempt to do. A flood of excitement raced through his heart.

"Wait," he said and pulled a lock of hair down over his eyes. It was blue. *Hey, I'm getting good at this.*

He replaced his hand underneath the edge of the couch and remembered the night before and how lifting those massive wooden beams hadn't been that difficult at all. And, he guessed, those beams weighed more than this couch. *But this is just for starters. No sense attempting something I don't think I can do.*

"Okay, here we go." He took a full breath, held it a second, exhaled and . . . lifted.

The couch flipped onto its back, as if four or five guys had been on the other side and suddenly pulled and slammed it down. The rear of the couch banged into the floor with a resounding *thud* and Gabriel's first thought was that the wooden floor beneath the carpet had been shattered.

"Nonononono . . ." He went to the other side and, much to his relief, found the backend of the couch sitting flush on the floor, the carpet—and presumably the wood underneath—intact and undamaged.

"Let's try that again," he said and dug his fingers underneath the couch's backside. This time, he exercised care and controlled the lift. Setting the couch back right-side-up took next to no effort at all even though he had to quickly put a hand against the cushion so as to slow the couch's descent back on its legs.

"Man," he whispered, "if I could just—"

Feeling like a puppy chasing its tail, he went back to the couch's front, got in position, this time sliding his palms passed the edge till they were around a third of the way toward the back.

"Go slow. Careful."

Gently, he pressed upward, his palms digging into the metal framing underneath. The whole couch lifted several inches off the floor.

Gabriel's breathing quickened.

The couch felt light, and though his brain knew better, knew he shouldn't have been able to lift it up on his own, he found himself slowly coming around to the reality before him. A big grin curled across his face.

He slid his hands under a little further until the front edge of the couch was sitting in the crooks of his elbows, its front end flush with his biceps. It was like balancing a large cardboard box filled with blankets.

Slowly, he began to stand. The couch rocked side to side like a teeter-totter. Carefully, he widened his grip to keep it balanced. Still smiling (he couldn't help himself), he stood up straight, his mind reeling with the idea that his leg strength must have been *gifted* by the messenger as well.

Standing upright, balancing the couch in his arms, he checked the distance between the couch and the ceiling.

FIRST NIGHT OUT

There was only about six inches till the couch's headrest would smack into it. Carefully, he raised the couch even more, ever mindful of the short amount of space he had to work with. Lifting it those remaining few inches didn't take much effort at all. It was like lifting a ten-or-fifteen pound chair shoulder height.

He stood there for a long time, constantly checking either end of the couch, marveling at its bottom hovering about five feet from the floor.

I could stand here all day like this, if I had to. The thought came out of the nowhere but it was, nonetheless, true.

Gabriel remained standing, couch in arms, for several more minutes before slowly setting it back down. Even readjusting his arms and hands on its descent was relatively easy now.

Once it was down, he took a step back and felt his forehead. It was dry.

"Hm, no sweat," he said with a wry grin. "That's gotta be, what, a few hundred pounds?" And he knew he could lift more.

Chapter Two

GABRIEL RAIDED HIS cupboards and fridge and loaded the couch cushions up with anything he could find: canned soups and vegetables, a jug of milk, a large sack of flour, a four-kilogram bag of sugar, a tub of ice cream—anything that weighed at least a pound or more. When he was done, the couch was a mess, covered with a mass of goods that made it look like countless grocery bags had exploded on top of it.

That's probably a hundred pounds more, he thought, surveying his work. "Might as well give it a try."

Like before, he positioned himself at the couch's center, squatted down and got his hands as far under the bottom as he could. Being mindful of the need to keep it all balanced lest the food topple off the couch, he slowly lifted and was surprised to find just a slight difference in the weight. He brought the couch up shoulder height then set it back down, wanting more of a challenge.

I need to know what my limits are, if I have any. And he hoped he did. The notion of having limitless strength, as cool as that would be, also set his heart racing. It wasn't so much the responsibility that came with such an ability, but more so the idea of *what* he'd have to find to lift to verify it was real. A car? A bus? Who knew?

He scanned the apartment. "Ah," he said, looking at the TV. It was a twenty-seven-incher with all its weight in the front. It had been a two-man job when moving in. He rearranged the goods on the couch, putting what he thought would be around fifty pounds worth of food on either side. Then he crossed the room, unplugged the TV from the wall, DVD player and VCR and MTS box, and wrapped his arms around either side of the large television set.

This isn't as heavy as you think it is, he told himself. And with that, he lifted . . . and stumbled back a few steps, putting more effort into it than he needed to.

Carefully, he turned around and gently set the TV on the couch. Taking a step back, he said, "That's probably, what, five-fifty, six hundred?" It could have been more, but a ballpark figure would be good enough for now.

"Okay, here we go again," he said and got himself situated in front of the couch. The moment he got his hands under, the TV on top of the cushions rocked a little. He shot an arm out to catch it and adjusted it so it leaned against the backrest. *Should have flipped it so the screen faced the other way. Aw well.* At least this way it would be more of a challenge which, he figured, would be a good thing. There was strength in balance, after all.

Gabriel put his hands where they needed to be and, shaking his head so a lock of blue hair fell before his eyes, began to lift.

The couch rose from the floor, teetering a bit to the left, then to the right. Cautiously, he adjusted his hands underneath, making sure it didn't dip too far one way or the other. Chuckling at the thought of what this would look like if someone walked in on him, he positioned his arms like he had before, the couch's edge sitting comfortable in the crooks of his elbows, his biceps up against its front.

"And up we go," he said and lifted. The couch rose higher until the top of the TV hit the ceiling with a plastic *bump*. "Whoops."

He hefted the weight. Not bad. Felt like he was holding a box full of books above his head, maybe sixty to seventy pounds for a normal person.

"More," he said and lowered the couch. When its legs touched the carpet, the hard thud it gave off really made it hit home how much he was lifting.

Over the next half hour or so, he experimented by adding more weight, rearranging things as needed. He added everything from shampoo and conditioner bottles to a stack of magazines to every book in the apartment. He even went so far as throwing his computer on top of there, printer and all. With each lift, it grew heavier, but not enough to make him want to quit. It got to the point that he had so much stuff on there that some of it rolling off was inevitable so he went to the closet, pulled out a couple of blankets, and put them over everything like a tarp. He fastened the blankets' edges to the front, back and sides of the couch with safety pins, just enough to catch something if it moved and allow him enough time to set the couch down before something got damaged.

By the time he put the couch down again, he estimated the whole thing probably weighed somewhere around eight hundred pounds, give or take. And that last lift took some effort, the resistance of the weight increasing its press against him the higher he lifted.

"This is crazy," he said. Then, with a grin, "I *need* to know."

What was strange was that he wasn't even tired. Though he was slowing down a bit, he was nowhere near the fatigue level he would normally feel after rearranging and moving everything around.

FIRST NIGHT OUT

The minutes went by quickly as he removed all that he had put upon the couch. But there was one more thing he could add: the recliner chair that matched the hide-a-bed. He picked up the chair, set it on top, then went about putting everything else back on top of the couch until what stood before him was a pyramid of odds and ends. He locked the blankets back in place and got ready.

As he squatted before the couch, his heart leapt within him and the excitement which signaled the onset of his powers came on full force. During all this experimenting, he had nearly forgotten his powers had been *on* the whole time. It could have been the anxiety for this next lift that did it, but bright blue light pooled in his eyes.

And he was staring straight at the center of the blanket where, underneath, sat his chair with the TV on top of it.

Clenching his teeth and furrowing his brow, he drew his focus onto what was happening, watched as the blue light covered his vision, erasing from existence the deep green blanket before him.

I will not let this overrule me, he thought. *This is mine.*

The light grew brighter and brighter and, judging by the energy beams' performance the night before, it'd only be a few seconds before a sharp blast shot out and destroyed what took him months of saving up to afford. There were only two ways out of this: either turn his powers off . . . or control them.

He kept his focus on the blue light, and willed it to remain where it was. He imagined invisible arms reaching out from the corners of his eyes and wrapping themselves around the energy that begged to be released.

"No," he said quietly. "No."

Attention solely on the blue light, he mentally told it to remain where it was . . . then grow brighter.

Stay. The light grew brighter and it felt as if a slight burst sparkled around his eyes. *Stay.* It grew brighter still and let off an even wider-arced burst. *Staaaay.*

The light remained where it was, blocking out everything but that brilliant blue.

He narrowed his eyes then imagined those invisible arms drawing the energy back in further and further until his vision finally began to clear. Slowly at first, then quickly.

Lips pursed, he let out a long exhale, not having realized he had been holding his breath.

He remained there before the couch for a time, making sure his eyes wouldn't flare up again.

The minutes trickled by and he wasn't sure how much time passed before he shook his head as if coming out of a daze.

"Man . . ." he whispered.

Hands ready, he re-focused on the task at hand . . . and lifted.

Grunting, he fought against the force pushing down against him. Breathing deep, he lifted the couch with everything on top of it until he was standing. The couch tipped to the side. He pushed up with his right hand. It tipped to the left. He pushed up with the opposite hand and got things level. That chair really made a difference.

Slowly, he crept his hands one at a time under the couch until they pressed firmly up against the center of the metal framing beneath, and set the couch securely against his arms as well. The sheer weight of the thing dug into the crook of his elbow and the way the weight of the front pressed into him made his arms feel like they were falling asleep.

Grimacing, and shoving any thoughts of putting it back down out of his mind, he lifted upward, fighting it inch by inch until the back of the chair touched the ceiling.

He held it there . . . and waited.

The massive weight of just over a thousand pounds obeyed the gravity that ruled the earth, pushing against him, the bottom of the hide-a-bed yearning to touch the floor once more.

"Keep it steady," he growled. The couch teetered to either side, and righting it put strain on his hands and wrists.

Breathing in slow then exhaling just as slowly, he smiled at the power that was a part of him.

Just over a thousand pounds. One. Thousand. That was half a ton.

That was the weight of some tractors.

His imagination kicked in and he imagined holding a John Deere in his arms, cradling it like a child.

The weight pressed down against him, but he held it there.

Time rolled by and it wasn't until the muscles in his arms and shoulders began to heat up that he slowly readjusted his hands and began to lower it.

He must have gotten the angle wrong because a few inches from the floor, his arms were situated as such that he couldn't put it down without dropping it the remaining distance.

"Oh, great," he said.

With a grunt, he slowly lifted the half-ton, object-laden couch higher until he was standing again. He readjusted his hands and arms and ignored the pain when the hard bottom edge of the right side of the couch plowed into the crook of his elbow.

"Agh!" he shouted. *Careful! Don't* . . . "Don't drop it."

Slowly, biting back the sharp pain at the base of his bicep, he managed to lower it . . . and set it down.

He fell back off his haunches and landed on his bottom. Gabriel remained sitting there, arms palm-upward at his sides, the insides of his hands and tops of his wrists beet red and throbbing, absorbing the moment.

One thousand pounds.

———

There was no room to run. And if Gabriel was to fly again, he *had* to run. Last night, that was how he had achieved flight. The energy within—the *excitement* that seemed to be the root of all this, the source of his power—had propelled his legs down the city streets, to the Forks and, when he reached the top of the stairway there, he had been able to leap down all eleven steps without twisting an ankle or, worse, breaking it. And it didn't end there. Once he was on the walkway alongside the Assiniboine River, his feet had left the ground and the night sky grew ever closer.

But it all began with running and in his one-bedroom apartment, he had all of fifteen feet or so in his front room to trot along, most of which was occupied with furniture and electronics.

I can try just running a few steps and see if that works, he thought. But deep down inside, he knew those couple of strides wouldn't be enough to give him the lift he needed.

"Am I supposed to run every time?" he said. *It would be pretty stupid if that's how it was. Yet again, flight is flight, which is just too cool on its own.*

The thought of waiting till dark and going for a run to test out the ability crossed his mind. But he couldn't wait.

Not since he had gotten a decent handle on his first two powers.

The apartment was dimly lit, the only light that which seeped through the cracks in the blinds over his balcony window.

"I can do this," he said.

He glanced around the room, taking note that all his belongings had been put back where they originally were. The notion of rearranging the furniture and TV, picking them up and setting them down, each object as light as a stack of blankets, crossed his mind, but even if he did so, it wouldn't free up much more room.

Flight.

He could master it.

Okay, you need "lift," he told himself. *Easy enough.* And it made sense. The idea of running so fast, the wind parting around him as his body pierced the air, the feeling of running so quickly that he could *catch up* with the wind and ride on top of it made him wonder if that was how this part of his power worked.

"Or maybe that's not it at all? The need to run could be psychological. I don't know." He took a deep breath, calming the heart that beat rapidly in anticipation of what was to come. "Well, might as well try. Do what works then go from there."

He backed up all the way to the front door. From here, there was a straight line running through his front landing and into his living room. Probably twenty-five to thirty feet, was his best guess. Should be enough to get things going.

Gabriel verified the door's deadbolt was locked then pressed his back and heels up against the door as much as he was able, palms flat against the wood. Shifting inside, he let the excitement fill him and grinned at the surge of energy that filled him to his core.

"On the count of three," he said. "One. Two. Three." He pressed off the door and ran till he was a few feet into his living room and leapt into the air.

He rose about three feet before his heels landed back on the carpet with a dull *thump!*

Okay. That didn't work. He checked his hair to make sure his powers were activated. They were.

"Let's try again," he said and trudged back toward the door.

Thinking that standing up against the door had hindered the initial burst of speed needed to engage in the run, this time he stationed himself in front of the door, left foot forward, bent at the knee, the other back, only slightly bent, like a runner on its mark.

He doubled checked his hair again. Still blue.

"Okay, powers are on. You've done this before. Do it again."

He focused on the spot on the carpet a few feet into his living room where he planned to jump from.

"One. Two. Three!" He took off again, hit the spot on the carpet and jumped. Once more he came back down, after gaining even less air than last time.

Growling in frustration, he turned to go back to the door then stopped himself. "You're making this too complicated. You've probably psyched yourself out. Last night you just did it. You didn't think. You only *did*. Do it again." The immediate retort: *Heh, easier said than done.* "I can do this. Don't think. Just do." *Where's that messenger when you need him?*

Gabriel crouched down and placed the bottoms of his forearms on the tops of his knees, trying to recall how it felt last night each time he took flight. The only thing the two take offs seemed to have in common was he had been running. But there had to have been something *more* to it, right? Something deeper? Or, maybe, not *as* deep?

He resolved to stay crouching there until the answer came to him as a self-imposed lesson in patience. He would figure this out.

Clearing his mind, he let his mind drift to the night before and replayed each take off over and over in his mind. Running, running, sprinting, flight. Running, running, sprinting, flight. All he had cared about during those moments was getting into the air. And something else had been there, too, another feeling or bit of knowledge. He just couldn't place it.

Running, running, sprinting, flight. Running, running, sprinting, flight.

Running, running—

The muscles around his eyes loosened and a subtle smile crept across his face when he realized what had been present last night and what was missing now.

Trust.

Complete and utter trust, one that manifested itself when he took off at the lakeshore. One so deep, so imbedded within him, he just simply believed he'd take to the air without second thought.

He just simply *did*.

"That's it," he whispered. "Trust." Gabriel stood and took a few steps so he was in the center of his living room. "Just simple trust. All I have to do is believe that it can be done. No thoughts of defeat, no thoughts of it not being possible. I did it before. I can do it again. Trust."

Heart thumping fast and quick, he took a deep breath and let out a slow exhale.

He didn't even check his hair. He didn't need to. He had to believe his powers were still on.

Trust, he thought, the word and calming feeling it inspired drawn out slowly in his mind and heart. *Trust. Just believe.*

Gabriel let his hands fall to his side, closed his eyes . . . and waited.

And waited.

And waited.

Just believe.

Rise up.

Trust.

The air pooled beneath his feet, tickling the skin.

The rush of air sweeping over his hands, the sides of his neck and his face told him everything.

He didn't have to look down to know his feet weren't touching the ground.

CHAPTER THREE

IN HINDSIGHT, STAYING in all day to practice flying was the right thing to do, especially since last night Gabriel had a hard time stopping his ascent the first time he floated into the sky. When the same thing happened a couple of times throughout the course of the day, he was grateful the ceiling stopped him from going any further.

Stopping only once for a brief snack, the entire day was spent practicing floating off the ground without the aid of a pre-flight run. He had tried defying gravity from a variety of positions, everything from simply standing erect to lying face down on the carpet so his body was automatically horizontal when he rose, to stepping off his couch and feeling nothing but air beneath his feet.

At first, getting himself to rise off the floor took focus and effort, but with each successful attempt, each subsequent effort grew easier and easier till, just after 5 P.M., all it took was the inner desire to fly to get himself into the air. He had practiced just merely floating, his body a few feet from the floor of his living room, to flying from one end of his suite to the other, his back occasionally bumping and scraping against the ceiling. One thing he learned was that just because your body was horizontal to the ground, that in and of itself didn't ensure a straight and level flight. No matter how many times he tried, he couldn't get his body *exactly* parallel to the floor. Instead, with each pass of the apartment, he had to work on leveling out when he dipped down too far or rose up too high and smashed into the ceiling.

It wasn't until 9 P.M. that he decided it was safe enough to go out without being seen.

Gabriel dressed in a gray sweat suit and got his runners on at the door. When he stood and looked at himself in the hallway mirror, he practiced *shifting* one more time, a "double check" to make sure that he was able to activate his powers when *he* commanded it, not them turning on when he wasn't ready for them.

Standing there, gazing at himself in the mirror, he felt his shoulders sink when he realized he couldn't just go out looking the way he did. Surely a man with brilliant and completely blue eyes and blue-sheened hair would stand out amongst everyone else out there.

"So what am I supposed to do, put a bag over my head?" he said. He actually entertained the idea of cutting a few holes in a garbage bag and using that to conceal himself before realizing that a guy walking around with a black plastic bag over his head would command as much attention as one with blue hair. "I need a mask." Except, he didn't have one. There was nothing he owned that he could use to cover his face. No old Halloween costumes, no balaclava for the winter. Nothing.

He powered down; a flash of blue cracked before his vision, the sign his powers had just left him. He opened the hall closet and rummaged through the items on the top shelf, seeing if there was anything up there that might be of some use. The closest thing he had to a balaclava was a deep navy toque. It would still keep his face exposed. What if he flipped the flap down and cut holes just above the edge, making it a mask? He took it down and looked it over.

FIRST NIGHT OUT

"Too obvious," he said. He wringed the toque a few times in his fingers then set it back on the shelf. "Wait."

Shoved way back in the corner of the shelf was a pair of old sunglasses, a pair he'd had since his early teens, with thick, black frames and scratched-up silvery lenses. He had stopped wearing them because he thought the large and curved lenses made him look like a fly.

He reached for them and the toque and pulled them down. "What if I take these *and* this?" he said, the glasses in one hand, the toque in the other.

He put the toque on then the shades, shoving the glasses' arms beneath the toque and over his ears.

Checking himself in the mirror, he realized he didn't look bad at all. He'd seen guys all the time walking around with sunglasses and a toque (especially in Winnipeg where folks seemed to wear toques year round regardless if there was snow or not). Wearing sunglasses at night seemed kind of stupid, but he didn't think anybody would give two hoots about it. He'd seen guys wearing shades in the late hours of the evening countless times. (He also always thought those guys looked ridiculous because it was nigh impossible to see anything when you wore shades at night.)

"This is as good as it's going to get," he said.

He took off the sunglasses, bent the arms and hung them on the collar of his shirt. He'd put them on when it was time. At least this way he could save face a little bit and not appear out of place unless he absolutely had to (and that was only if anyone was around).

Gabriel grabbed his keys, turned off the lights to his place, and exited the apartment.

He had work to do.

———

Gabriel wondered at each face he passed as he walked down the street. Did any of them have a clue as to what was passing by them? Did they have any idea that the young man in the dark navy toque and gray sweat suit was capable of more than they ever dreamed? Was there any inkling that in the days and weeks to come, their world could change forever based on what he decided to do with these abilities?

It was that latter question that hung over him. The options were almost limitless. So much power, so much potential. Once he fully mastered these abilities, the world would become his playground and, if he played his cards right, he could have anything he wanted. Everyone would love him. People looked up to sports stars, models and actors all the time. They couldn't possibly treat someone with supernatural abilities any differently. No longer would he be Gabriel Garrison the forgotten one. No longer would he have to live life on the sidelines, watching as everyone else got a break and got what they wanted. And no longer would he be alone. Friends, girls, money—anything was possible.

But only if he was careful in his execution.

Time would tell.

Gabriel rounded a corner at the end of the street, went about seven blocks, then turned down the back alley of a string of apartments.

The alley was empty.

He walked down halfway, keeping constant watch for anyone out for a late evening stroll. Aside from a couple of cats, not a living soul was present.

Good, he thought.

He put the sunglasses over his eyes and walked a bit further, allowing his eyes to adjust to the dark as best as they could. A minute later, and it was still hard to see. But when he looked up at the night sky, the moon shone bright despite the darkness the lenses enforced.

Peeking over the frames for a clear view, Gabriel checked up and down the alley, then the windows of the surrounding apartment blocks looking out over the street. A few windows were dark, a few others the same but with blinds drawn. Others had lights on, but the blinds down and closed. Only one window had a light on and the blinds open, but no one was there.

"So it starts now," he said quietly. *Okay, just like you practiced.*

Gabriel *shifted* inside, reveling in the immediate warmth of the all-encompassing energy that flooded through him.

He turned his face toward the sky, raised his arms, his fingers together, pointing upward.

Just like it had been in his apartment, all he had to do was rise up on his toes and press off against the ground with the balls of his feet. And he was airborne.

The wind flowed over and around him, bathing him with a cool breeze and the fresh scent of night air.

Rebirth. Like it was last night, like it was today each time his body left the ground.

The moon shone through the dark lenses of his shades, a full circle of off-white with dark gray craters. He wiggled his fingers, imagining himself touching it.

Up he rose, higher and higher, nothing but air around him and the freedom it ensured. Some would say that flying so high, just you and nothing else, was what loneliness was all about. Instead, Gabriel found himself at home in the sky, as if he was somehow meant to live up here above it all.

He had dreamed of flying before, but even on those few occasions where he imagined himself soaring through the clouds, there was still the niggling feeling deep in his consciousness that that wasn't how it was supposed to be, that people weren't meant to fly.

Up here, the ground and city streets distancing themselves further and further away from him, that feeling of the abnormality of flight was absent. Completely.

Perhaps it had been the full day of experimenting with his powers, perhaps it was the surrealness of it all that overrode everything, but right now, nothing felt more natural than floating into the night.

He glanced down and could only guess as to how high he was. Maybe a couple of thousand feet. Maybe a bit more. Maybe a bit less. He allowed himself to rise a few moments more before bending forward at the waist, leveling himself out so his feet and legs were now behind him, his heels at first fighting against the air that threatened to push his legs down. Once more or less on his stomach, he immediately shot forward. The mental image of air blasting forth from the bottoms of his feet flashed before his eyes. Though he felt nothing coming out of his feet, perhaps in some way that was how his flight power functioned: a kind of self-propulsion, his body generating the bursts of air needed to keep himself aloft.

Racing through the sky, Gabriel chuckled as the wind tickled his chin and the sensitive skin of his lips. He dipped his head low so it was between his outstretched arms. The wind blowing into the top of his head flowed through the pores in the toque's fabric, through the strands of hair, licking his scalp. It was cold and refreshing, icy and invigorating.

FIRST NIGHT OUT

The distant ground—nothing but a blur of murky rooftops—passed by slowly beneath him. If he was flying lower, he figured, they'd probably zip by. Everything seemed to move slower the higher you went. He knew as much from the one flight he took back in grade seven from Winnipeg to Chicago with his family.

He looked up; a low-hanging cloud, thin and wispy, floated before him. He went into it, his sight immediately stolen in the cloud's dark gray, the lenses of his glasses fogging up from the moisture. When he emerged on the other side, he hesitated before removing his glasses, not wanting to somehow lose concentration on what he was doing and fall toward the earth. Carefully, he took the sunglasses from his eyes, slowly brought them to his shirt then quickly rubbed the lenses against the fabric. Without the lenses' dark shade over his eyes, he couldn't help himself but let his jaw fall open at the nearly-clear sky before him. Fine pin pricks of sparkling yellow light coated the night sky's purply-black canvas. The moon was white and full, like a second sun this high up. Tears welled in his eyes at the sight. Unlike last night, now that he was more comfortable with his powers, he could really take it all in and appreciate the magnificence of a night sky for what it really was. Utterly beautiful, awe-inducing and inspiring.

Who was he to have been chosen to experience this? Why him out of all the men on the earth? What did the messenger see in him that made him stand out among the rest? Surely it couldn't have been anything special. Years of rejection and consistent feelings of inadequacy ruled that out. But there had to be something, right? Unless, maybe, he had been chosen at random and this was the result of some cosmic gamble he knew nothing about.

Maybe this was all a test, to see what he'd do with his abilities once he mastered them? And if he made the wrong choice—whatever that might be—maybe they'd be taken away? There was no way to know and, Gabriel figured, there was no way he *could* know save another meeting with that nameless figure made of brilliant blue light.

I hope I make the right decision, whatever that is, he thought.

He couldn't help the sickening feeling that crept into his stomach, the idea—and almost foreknowledge—that he *would* make the wrong choice and, like most everything else he had ever aspired to or attempted to do with his life, he'd miss out because he didn't have what it took to see something through to correct completion.

"I hope not," he said quietly. *But it won't surprise me if it pans out that way.*

Tears welled up in his eyes anew, this time not from the stunning display of creation before him.

"I better do the right thing," he muttered.

He wiped the glasses one more time on his sweater then brought them to his face. When he put them back on, he didn't mind that he hadn't done a thorough job at cleaning them, but at least now he could see more clearly.

He banked sharply to the left—a little too sharply—and almost did a three-hundred-sixty-degree turn.

"Try again," he said, and attempted the bank once more. This time, more focused, he turned only to the left, aligning himself more rightly with the city.

Aiming his hands high, he arced his body . . . and climbed into the sky. A gust of cold current shot at him, blowing him backward in a somersault. The world went topsy-turvy—ground then sky, ground then sky—until he was facing upward, his belly toward space . . .

. . . and dropping.

Arms and legs flailing instinctively, he could already feel the sudden *WHAM* of his back hitting the ground then, after that, the fleeting thought that he *wouldn't* feel the impact and would die instantly.

"Ohmanohmanohmanohman . . . . Um, um, um . . ." His mind went blank and panic swept over him.

Heart beating so hard it wouldn't surprise him if it sprang forth from his chest and tumbled to the earth sometime after he became nothing more than mashed hamburger on the ground below, he fought the urge to scream, but found himself doing so anyway. A fall like this was something he hadn't practiced for.

The wind rushed past on either side like a blanket of air that wouldn't fully wrap itself around him.

He snapped his arms and legs out, making his body as flat as a board.

"Go forward," he shouted.

Air billowed up beneath him like a massive and plush cushion. His fall slowed some then with a violent jerk he darted forward, the stars above moving quick and out of his line of sight.

Breathing rapidly, Gabriel feared what might happen if he turned over. How far was he from the ground? If he lost control again, would there be enough time to right the situation and fly on or would death overtake him just as he almost had these powers figured out?

Not wanting to risk it, he summoned all the strength in his abdominal muscles, fought against the blanket of wind resistance above his face and chest, and sat up just enough to bow his body, arms still above his head. Now in the shape of an awkward U, the change in arm direction drew him upward at an angle, the wind kicking him forward. It took a moment but he righted himself and he flew toward the stars, his body straight up and down. He glanced at his feet and was thrilled to see he hadn't fallen all that far and still had a thousand or so feet to go before it would have been too late.

After obtaining a few hundred more feet of flight, Gabriel bent forward, leveled himself out, then banked right, heading back toward the city, using the two towers of the Richardson Building and CanWest Global Place as his landmarks.

Yet if he flew down and wove between the city streets, he wasn't sure he'd be able to handle the task without messing up. Worse, he wasn't sure if he was ready for anybody to see him yet.

The city got closer.

Chapter Four

It was tempting to swoop down and fly just above the cars and garner the attention of those strolling the sidewalks at this late hour. Gabriel even dipped his flight slightly for a moment, but arced back up when he realized that if he made a mistake, if he somehow lost control and either crashed into a car or truck or hit the pavement altogether, he'd be dead. And if he did somehow manage to survive the fall or vehicle impact, the thought of never ending questions and endless research on his body made him shudder. Worse, everyone would know who he was and, most likely, folks would crowd his parents' place "just for a little chat" and overflow Dolla-card with questions about its no-name customer service representative.

Gabriel flew higher and higher until the tops of the Richardson and CanWest Global Place buildings were a couple hundred meters below him. Surely no one would see his gray sweat suit zipping past the dark night sky even if they did look up.

Below, the city changed into suburbs and ruler-straight streets; the wind blew across his face, each gust of cool air a reminder of the freedom hugging the sky entailed.

He could stay up here for hours. He had probably been up here for over an hour already. He didn't know and, right now, didn't want to check his watch. To be on a clock at a time such as this . . . it didn't make sense. Freedom and power were not constrained by time or schedule. It lived its own life, had its own way.

It was its own world, and one Gabriel was beginning to feel at home in.

So, so fresh. So, so amazing.

Up here, there was no world, no life at some crummy call centre, no bills and no cares.

Glorious.

The blocky shadows that were the houses of suburbia below trickled away until Gabriel recognized that the long strip of gray lit up by bright dots of yellow on poles that looked like Q-tips below was Highway 59. He glanced over his shoulder. The building tops of downtown Winnipeg were mere silhouettes against the deep purple sky.

Out here, away from the city, there was no pressure. And if something should happen, there would be no one around to see it. Just like last night when flying above the train.

Gabriel flew on and settled his gaze on the murky patch of wavy gray off to the right. Spring Hill, or, at least, the small valley of sand hills and rocks next to it, called the Pits by some.

Though it had only been in the back of his mind, he knew there was still one more thing he had to do if he wanted to come away from tonight with a decent handle on his powers. With that thought in mind, he banked over to the Pits, mindful of the occasional car zipping along the highway.

Last night, when he had finally landed in the alley two streets over from his apartment building, he had managed to land somewhat properly, though the sudden impact wreaked havoc on his knees. He hoped he could duplicate either that or manage a better landing tonight.

Or break my legs, he thought.

Remembering what helped him quicken and slow his flight from the night before, Gabriel bent his toes inward, pointing them toward his shins as much as he could. Last night, the maneuver helped him slow down whereas pointing his toes and flattening his feet helped him speed up.

Immediately, his flight began to slow. He angled his body downward toward the Pits, careful to come at it from the side opposite the highway lest anybody see him soar overhead. Wind rushed up to meet him as he slowed even more. Lower, lower, careful now. The ground quickly came up beneath him. He dropped his legs, his heels dangling a few feet from the ground. Lower and . . . *thoomp!* His legs bent the second he touched down and he stumbled a few steps forward. A better landing, but it still needed work. Gabriel remained there staring at his feet for a moment, centering himself before taking another step.

"Okay, I'm down," he said. He couldn't help but smirk when he noticed his arms were still held out straight in front of him, as if he were still in flight. "Also gotta work on not looking so dainty when I land, too."

The Pits were empty and void of all light save for the faint yellow glow coming from the top of Spring Hill some distance away. The streetlamps from the highway above and to the side only cast enough light for him to make his way around without tripping, but did not lend enough light for him to see clearly. He removed his sunglasses. Not much better, but enough to make do.

He counted off on his fingers: "Strength. Check. Turning powers on and off. Check. Flying. Check.

Landing. Half-check. Eye beams . . . quarter-check, I guess." *I can keep them at bay, but that's about it.*

With a nod to himself, he turned his back to the highway and marched into the dark. When far enough away to feel certain that no one driving by would see him, he stationed himself in front of the biggest mound of gravel and sand he could find, then stepped back about fifteen feet.

He double-checked the highway again and froze when he saw a few headlights coming from behind. Gabriel stood perfectly still, on the off chance those in the vehicles saw his movement and began to wonder what someone was doing alone down in the Pits late at night.

The cars finally passed and Gabriel didn't see any more coming.

Content the coast was clear, he focused his attention on the hill of sand before him and picked out a spot roughly at the hill's center for his target.

Just hope it's packed tight, he thought. He figured it should be. The huge hills of sand had been there for the longest time and, as much as he was able to surmise, hadn't changed much in size, if at all, in all these years.

He stared intently at the portion of sand, breathed in deep through his nose and exhaled slow through his mouth. Heart kicking into high gear, the excitement his powers generated blossoming, blue light filled the corners of his eyes. Never letting his eyes wander from the spot in the sand, he let the light grow and grow until it blanketed his vision. Everything was cast in a blue haze and he had to focus extra intently to keep the spot in the sand front and center.

Should I do a little bit at first or . . . But it was too late. The light grew in brightness, more and more, until all he saw was brilliant blue, as if staring straight on into a neon light bulb. In his mind's eye, he imagined those little arms on either corner of his eye sockets, the arms and hands acting as a net, keeping the power in.

Brighter and brighter, then a flash of even more dazzling light, almost white.

"Now!" he shouted without meaning to.

He widened his eyes, releasing the energized blue build up, sending forth two beams of raw power. The moment the beams left his eyes, his vision returned just enough for him to see the three-foot-long beams dart through the air and blast into the sand in a rough *FWOOM*. Sand shot out in all directions at the center of the hill and came down in gravelly rain. Smoke trickled out from the dark hole in the hill, as if someone had a secret bonfire going on within.

The sound from the blast—he hadn't expected it to be so loud, like a gunshot.

A part of him expected to hear the sound of screeching tires fill the air as those somewhere near on the highway heard the blast and came to see what it was about. Instead, silence hung on the air save for the sound of cars in the distance.

Gabriel trotted up to the smoking hole in the sand to inspect it. It was about a foot in diameter, its outer edge hard and smooth. The hole was dark, probably at least a foot or two deep. He ran his fingers along its edge and tugged them back at the heat he felt there. Hot glass, like a cup fresh from the dishwasher. He daren't stick his hand in to see exactly how deep it was while heat permeated off it like a furnace.

His mind went blank for a moment as he took it all in. He hadn't expected the sand to melt. Last night, when he had touched his power-filled eyes, it felt more like sticking your finger in an electrical socket. Now . . .

"It's based on intensity," he said quietly. *The more I hold it in, the more I let it grow, the hotter it gets.*

He took three long strides backward and repositioned himself in front of the sand hill. "I need to know."

The hole stood before him and as if the sight of the black hole beheld revelation, the excitement returned, his mind reeling over what he'd just accomplished. Blue light pooled around the corners of his vision and he allowed it to continue to do so until once more he was looking through a sheet of blue light.

He widened his eyes and two little balls of energy sped forth, dinging the sides of the hole in the sand in two tiny fireworks of glass.

"Hm, interesting."

Gabriel did it again, this time holding the light at bay and, cautiously, verified with a touch *what* this energy felt like when it wasn't filling his eyes full force. A jolt of electric power coursed through his fingers, the sharp tingle racing through the bones, up his hand and into his wrist and lower forearm. He shook his hand against the air from the sting.

But the light was still building and he understood that though the energy hurt his skin when he touched it, he didn't feel that sharp electric tingle in his eyes.

The light grew even brighter.

He widened his eyes and expelled it; two foot-long blasts plowed into the sand on either side of the hole, kicking up sand and gravel.

Chuckling, he did it again and again, varying how much of this awesome power he allowed to build up before sending it flying forward. Each blast was accompanied by a *crack*, sometimes loud, sometimes soft, depending on how much he let loose, and each *crack* was accompanied by a bright flash of blue.

FIRST NIGHT OUT

When he heard cars approaching, he stopped and waited. And when they cleared, he got back to work, varying the strength of each blast.

By the time he was done, over an hour had passed.

The hole that started out a foot in diameter was now a cavernous mouth large enough to swallow a man.

All smiles, he geared himself up for another shot.

The blue energy sped over his eyes, and it was then he noticed he could summon it forth at different intensities based on his desires. All it took was practice. That's all the other powers took, too. Practice.

The light covered his vision and Gabriel let it grow.

Brighter and brighter until all sight was blocked out by blue-white light. As he focused on harnessing it all in, every so often a stark white flash of light would flash over the blue, as if the power itself was begging him to let it go. But no, he wouldn't. Not until he knew *how much* power he had.

The blue light became a swirling mass of what appeared to be tiny blue flames, as if he were looking at the sun through a blue cellophane filter on a telescope. Bright—so bright he feared he might go blind.

A faint crackling filled his ears and when he reached his right hand up near his face, sharp and hot tingling licks of raw energy tickled his skin and singed his palm.

"Ow!" he shouted.

But he didn't let go.

Brighter. More power.

The crackling grew louder. And louder. And louder still.

A blinding flash of white burst before his eyes and he released.

BWOOM!

Thunder rang in his ears as two massive beams burst forth, each at least a foot around and five feet long, lighting up the sand hill and the hills on either side in blue light. The gigantic beams plowed into the vacuous black hole in the hill, decimating everything it touched. The small now-glass wall holding up the hill somewhere deep in the back blew away in a brilliant rainstorm of shimmering glass and dusty sand; gravity consumed the top of the hill and it fell to the earth. Dust kicked up everywhere and showered down in sandy glory.

Gabriel dropped to his knees and shielded his face and body with his arms as glass and sand sprayed at him. Tiny shards plowed into his sweatshirt, a few cutting through and zinging his skin. Eyes squeezed shut, he waited several moments for things to settle, then opened them and got to his feet in a rush when he heard squealing car tires and shouts from those on the highway not far away.

"Uhohuhohuhoh . . ." Blackness his only sight, he winced as he ran as fast as he could away from the highway, tripped a couple of steps and nearly took a tumble. Catching his balance, he threw his glasses on and tossed his hands up as he raced into the dark, unsure footing all the way.

Air swirled beneath his feet and Gabriel entered the sky, still partially blinded to all around him by the bright blue energy that had spilled forth from his eyes.

Hopefully no one saw him.

Chapter Five

Gabriel swept through the night, practicing straightening his toes and bringing them in, going faster, slowing down. Each moment that passed helped adjust his eyes to the night, his vision through the dark lenses of his sunglasses dim but not as blind as he had been when he took off.

Tomorrow's paper would tell if anyone saw anything, and if not tomorrow—as if they could ignore headline news like a man flying—then the day after.

He straightened his toes, brought them in; fast then slow, with each burst forward bringing a refreshing gust of wind.

Which makes we wonder how fast I can really go? he thought.

A thousand feet below, Highway 59 stretched on. There were only a few cars going in either direction on each of the dual-laned roadways. From what he recalled, the speed limit here was eighty kliks an hour, though most did eighty-five or ninety. From this high up in the sky, the cars appeared to be moving slower than they really were.

He dipped his hands and arced his body so he was more at an angle, kicked his heels up and dove toward the earth.

He was getting better at this; more at ease and more at home. A maneuver like that one last night or even earlier would have cost him. Now, though it took a conscious effort to right himself level at about two hundred feet up, it came easier.

The cars zipped by below, the sound of their tires racing along the pavement like a series of manila folders scraping along a wooden desk. Thinking the glare from the streetlamps was enough to hide him from any drivers or passengers below, Gabriel focused on keeping up with the cars.

Below and just behind him, a gray minivan moved along at a good clip and was probably doing the speed limit. Gabriel positioned himself so he was in line with it when it came up from behind. It passed by beneath him. He straightened his toes and welcomed the rush of the air that greeted him as he cut through the wind.

Jaw set, teeth and fists clenched, Gabriel forced his toes back as much as he could, moving and *willing* himself forward as quickly and as much as possible. For a brief moment he kept pace with the van until, slowly, it sped up ahead and was soon several meters in front. Then ten meters. Then twenty-five.

Not letting the vehicle out of his sight, he kept following it, forcing himself and *willing* himself to go as fast as he could, his only thought that of catching up to the van.

Push yourself! he barked inside. But no matter how hard he tried, how much he strained, he couldn't go any faster. Even his toes ached from being forced so far back and his shoulder and trapezoid muscles throbbed from all the stretching.

The train from last night. He had managed to keep up with that, but not this van.

FIRST NIGHT OUT

The minivan was over seventy meters ahead now, probably more, and would soon be too far away to continue pursuit.

The train. How fast did it go? Sixty kilometers an hour? Seventy? Somewhere around there, Gabriel guessed. He knew from riding alongside many trains with his father that they traveled around that fast, depending. And it was that speed he had managed last night.

He soared upward, calculating roughly how long it took for the minivan to move on ahead.

Sixty or so kilometers an hour as his top flight speed?

Seemed right.

———

The fatigue finally caught up to him. While Gabriel flew home with the refreshing night breeze blowing across his face, he felt like someone had suddenly robbed him of whatever strength his now-powerful muscles possessed. And for a moment—just a brief moment—he thought his powers had left him, that the messenger had reclaimed what he'd given. But that was only for a moment.

Gabriel returned to the alley he had taken off from earlier, his landing more or less polished, though he still stumbled a few steps forward on touchdown.

The walk back to his place seemed to take longer, which was strange because usually the trip *there* always seemed to take longer than the trip *home*. He didn't know why.

It was close to four in the morning when he unlocked the door to his suite. The thought of bed never felt so good. And rightly so. He had hardly slept the past couple of nights and had barely eaten anything, the anxiety over these new abilities having formed a swarm of butterflies in his stomach that would not be abated regardless of how hard he tried to slow down.

Home. His apartment seemed foreign now. Though deep within he knew that it was his, that it had finally taken on the penetrating feeling of home after having lived with his parents for over twenty years, now it seemed like it belonged to someone else. To a different Gabriel, a man who'd come to an end a little over twenty-four hours before.

"What are you talking about? You're still the same person," he said as he removed his toque, shades and runners. "Same guy. Same life. Just—" *Different.* He had never been one for change.

Though not the type to be rock hard set in his ways, the idea of things suddenly becoming different—especially when he had no control over it—he had never been good at that, at adjusting. And these powers . . . these powers meant change. A change for what, he didn't know, and the black and white question of whether for good or ill wasn't really the question either. It was more so their *effect* on his life and whether he'd be able to strike an even balance between any good or ill intentions that might arise.

He went to the bathroom and washed his hands. Out of habit, he glanced up to look at himself in the mirror and by its absence was reminded of how he'd accidentally destroyed it.

In the hall, Gabriel rubbed at the black smudge on the mirror with his sleeve. A bit of black came off, but not all and the mirror was warped where his eyebeams had struck. His hair still carried a blue sheen, his eyes large, sparkling blue marbles set in his head. Their bright glow was enough to hold his gaze, their stare mesmeric and penetrating. He was still amazed that though his eyes shone blue, he could see as clear as he did when his powers weren't activated.

Look at yourself, he thought. *As fun as all this is, this isn't normal. No one looks like this. No one can do what you do.* He took a deep breath, his heart hollow. *You're not human anymore.* Tears pricked at the corners of his eyes from the realization. *Not human.*

He needed the messenger.

Gabriel went to his computer, turned it on and did everything the same—from what he could remember—as the night the messenger first came to him.

Email inbox before him, he sat there and waited.

———

Gabriel awoke with a start, his legs jerking then kicking the row of power cords beneath his computer desk. Arms crossed and head bowed, it took him a moment to understand what he was looking at when his thighs blurred into view.

The clock on the right hand bottom side of the computer monitor read 6:42 A.M. He had been asleep for about two hours. Head throbbing with fatigue, his heart sank when only a plain email inbox was before him. No dance of amazing, bright blue lights and no messenger.

"Oh, man," he groaned quietly and unfolded his arms.

Stiff and sore, he stood, stretched, then walked slowly to the bathroom again. When he passed the hallway mirror, he noticed his hair was brown, his eyes back to normal. He was too tired to even bother trying to summon his powers again. Yet . . .

He *shifted,* and his eyes flared up with blue light, his hair coated with a blue sheen.

Still got 'em, he thought. He powered down and used the restroom. He emerged wearing only his boxers.

The thought of going to work today, though kind of appealing, made him realize he wasn't yet ready to face the world again. Once more the strong desire to call up his folks and tell them all about what happened surfaced. He shoved the thought and temptation away, knowing full well what such an act might lead to.

He still needed to figure this out.

In the kitchen, he picked up the phone and left another message for Rod, informing him he still wasn't feeling well and would be taking another day to rest up before returning to work tomorrow. He just hoped Rod would understand as his boss was the type who frowned on absences even when you had a good reason.

Gabriel hit the bedroom but not before stopping by the mirror one more time. Now, with his clothes off, he was able to look himself over—his upper body, anyway—and see if this newfound strength had somehow affected him physically. It hadn't. Though he wasn't out of shape by any means, there wasn't any noticeable change in his musculature. His arms—bearing a few red marks from when the blast of glass and sand hit him—were slightly defined, just like before, same with his chest and stomach. A few tiny lines of red were streaked across those as well. And, like before, he could see his ribcage slightly beneath his skin, mainly on the sides. He plucked a handful of teeny glassy shards from his skin that had cut through his sweatshirt. Wincing with each pull, he marveled that he hadn't noticed them in there all night. He checked himself over for any more bits of glass, straining when he had to reach around and feel his back.

FIRST NIGHT OUT

There didn't seem to be any more.

His legs were thin, with small calves. Perhaps, over time, with the continued use of his powers, he'd put on some muscle. Everywhere. Maybe.

There was still so much to learn.

When Gabriel got up around noon, he had a light breakfast then set about practicing the use of his powers again. Like yesterday, he practiced *shifting* back and forth, summoning the powers then letting them recede back inward. He repeated the lifting exercises, once more using his couch, chair, computer, printer, TV and all the other stuff. He practiced floating and leaving the ground without a running start as best he could in the tiny amount of space he had. Even on a dare with himself, he exercised filling his eyes with electric light then letting it recede, each go at it one more step closer to mastering the art of controlling the most deadly of his gifts. Everything he did verified the discoveries made the previous day. The only thing he wanted to try again was testing his top flight speed, but he'd wait until dark for that.

At night, he donned the sweat suit again and put on the toque and shades. Figuring that for now sticking to habit was the best way to ensure the safety and secrecy of his new abilities, he once more hoofed it the seven blocks over to that alley and tore into the sky as fast as he could when he was sure no one was looking. He also figured that, after buying a copy of the *Free Press* and the *Sun* from the red and blue dispensers in his front lobby, and they didn't report anything from the night before, he was safe. Might as well run with what worked until proven differently or, at least, until you think you could handle a change.

Tonight, flying was like being reacquainted with an old friend and Gabriel took comfort that this skill was slowly becoming a habit instead of the exploration of a brand new ability with each outing. And like the night before, he used the traffic on the highway to gauge his speed as best he could. He once ventured to flying high over a suburban area where the speed limit was fifty and was pleased to find he could pass the cars below, at least from a few hundred feet up. Estimating his top flight speed at around sixty or so kilometers an hour seemed right. If he was proven wrong in the future, so be it, but for now, it was good to at least have a baseline of some kind to operate from.

What about pairing a few abilities up? he wondered. He figured he was ready, or more or less comfortable enough to focus on more than just one of his powers.

Gabriel soared high into the sky and burst through a series of low-hanging clouds, bringing forth the power into his eyes and letting the blue pool up until he could no longer see what was before and under him. Not giving in to the instinctive bout of panic that swept over him, he let the energy build up even more until bright blue light became everything. With a power burst, he shot the beams forward. With a loud *crack*, they raced through the sky and shot into the night. If anyone saw that below, they would think it a flash of lightning, nothing more. Up here, he was safe.

Chuckling and thrilled that he seemed to have a pretty good handle on this, he fired off blast after blast, experimenting with their length and intensity.

"Not bad at all," he said after a time.

It was time for the next combo.

FIRST NIGHT OUT

A few minutes later, he landed in a small patch of forest just outside the city.

Selecting a thick tree about twenty-five feet high, he wrapped his arms around it low on the trunk and hugged it hard. The right side of his face planted firmly against the rough bark, he silently counted to three . . . and lifted.

The tree shook in its place then tipped slightly away from him as it began to break free from the earth. Gabriel hung on and straightened it as best he could to keep the gigantic thing balanced.

The lower base of the tree trunk lifted about half a foot from the earth, its roots coming with it, the long ropes of wood tearing up the ground all around. He didn't know one of the roots was just under his foot and when it kicked up beneath the arch, it sent him stumbling back a couple of steps. The tree toppled toward him, nearly taking him down with it. He fought against the momentum and pushed in the opposite direction, righting it once more.

"Now's the time to see if I can do this," he said. And with that, his feet left the ground and he ascended into the sky, taking the huge tree with him.

The ground rumbled below as the roots tore from the soil. The loud dusty shower of dirt rained down as the final portions of the tree broke free and floated into the sky, leaving a deep black hole and tossed and ripped up earth below.

At first the lift demanded effort, but once he was a few hundred feet up, it was as if the tree had suddenly become lighter on its own.

Gabriel was far enough out of range of the eyes and ears of the city—even the highways—that he didn't worry about anybody seeing a tree flying in the sky. When he was about five hundred feet up, he adjusted his hold on the tree so it sat cradled in his arms like an adoring bride. Gabriel slowly inched his way along its shaft, placing himself more in its center. A couple of times the bark scraped the fabric of his sweatshirt and he thought he heard the material tear once or twice. No matter. This had to be done.

Occasionally, his mind desired to focus on a single ability, but he forced his attention to divide between the two: strength and flight. And after a few minutes of flying through the sky away from the city, doing these two tasks simultaneously became almost second nature. Almost. He still had to remind himself of *what* he was doing and be consciously aware of the job at hand.

The tree sat solidly in his arms the higher he flew and when there was only endless field below, Gabriel readied himself for the final step in what he knew he needed to do tonight before he went home.

Double checking the expanse of dark gray field below, the night sky open and clear of any birds or even aircraft, Gabriel repositioned his hands beneath the tree so he held it aloft in his palms, elbows bent, the trunk up against his chin. He could barely see over it.

With a powerful push, he sent the tree hurtling up and into the air in a huge arc. It took several seconds before it reached its apex and began coming down. Gabriel flew after it as it descended and when he was about thirty feet away, he powered up his eyes and sent a mighty blast of raw energy at the tree. The blue beams of light streaked through the sky and zapped the treetop, blasting branches and leaves into a shimmering rain of splinters and sawdust.

The other half spun off to the side when torn from its counterpart. Gabriel took off after it, arms outstretched, fists clenched, eyes set on the tree's base and stringy umbrella-like structure of its roots. Fixing the roots in his line of vision, he sent off another shot of electric power, destroying it.

A portion of the trunk still fell toward the earth.

Gabriel flew after it, came up under it, hoping to catch it—and slammed into it instead, knocking his face against the bark, a dry, echoey *thwunk* shooting from his forehead to the back of his skull.

"Agh!" he cried. His sunglasses were cracked and the bridge of his nose hurt from where the plastic bridge of the glasses banged into it.

Hands still empty, he searched below for the falling tree. He didn't see its shadowed form against the dark.

Hopefully it found a home in a field below and didn't hit anything.

Chapter Six

THE BUS RIDE to work the next day was mind-numbingly slow. How easy it would have been to throw on the toque and sunglasses and a hoody, and fly over the buildings and get there in a quarter of the time.

But, one thing at a time, he thought as he sat in the crowded bus. The seats were filled; same with the aisle. Most folks had a drab expression on their face, as if each one wasn't thrilled to be going to the office today.

Gabriel felt the same way.

It wasn't that he didn't like his job. It wasn't the greatest thing in the entire universe, being a customer service representative for a credit card company, but it wasn't entirely terrible either. It paid enough to live on and he spent the majority of his days behind a desk, sitting down. Even now, at twenty-four, he'd now and then see other guys and girls he went to school with doing jobs that were far more physically demanding— pumping gas, waiting tables, bartending. To make a living sitting down wasn't too bad at all. But now, with these powers . . . did he really *have* to work? Couldn't he do something with them, something that would make his life, at least financially, easier?

The thick-faced gentleman sitting beside him coughed but didn't cover his mouth. Gabriel made a face. *Thanks a lot, buddy. Didn't your momma ever teach you*—The bus was almost at his stop. Gabriel pulled the cord and squeezed his way into the aisle so he could get off, only to be met by unfriendly stares from those standing who had to squish up against each other so he could get by.

After the bus stopped and he de-boarded, he joined the crowd on the sidewalk and headed toward the Dolla-card building.

His powers.

No matter what I use them for, it would mean I'd have to reveal to everyone else what I can do, he thought. He stopped short at the next thought and a middle-aged lady walking behind him bumped into him. She gave him an angry glare and pushed past him. *If I show myself . . . . I . . . I don't think I'm ready for that yet.* He began walking again. *Yet.*

Gabriel entered the front doors to Dolla-card and rode the elevator up to the seventh floor. He swiped his pass card in the slot by the doors leading to the calling floor and aside from offering a few good morning nods, went to his desk without talking to anybody.

As his computer booted up for the day, he pulled his pen out from the front pocket of his white collared shirt, then set his gaze on the thighs of his black dress pants. He hated wearing these clothes and avoided dressing up as much as possible. Thank goodness Dolla-card's dress policy was business casual and the most he'd ever have to worry about were dress pants and collared shirts or sweaters. No ties, no jackets. Only when higher-ups came for a tour was formal attire required.

Just before he placed his headset on, he tugged his bangs down so he could see them; a precaution to verify his powers hadn't shifted on without his knowledge, though if he had accidentally activated them, someone would have surely said something by now.

He got his screens ready and took his first call.

The morning wore on. Slowly. Each second that passed seemed like a minute. Each minute, nearly an hour. Though he had had slow days before, none of them compared to today. All he wanted was to log off and head home and experiment with his powers again. Instead, he was stuck here earning his daily bread because he couldn't afford any unpaid days off and he had already used two sick days in a row. If he had used three, Dolla-card's policy dictated he'd need a sick note from his doctor to explain his absence. But the thought of seeing Dr. Ruben before knowing how or if these new abilities revealed themselves in his body, even when they were in recession, made Gabriel's stomach stir. There would be no telling what Dr. Ruben's discovery of these powers would lead to and Gabriel had seen enough movies to know that those who were "special" were always carted off to some secret testing facility for study.

He hoped the policy wouldn't change and he'd need a note even for a single day off.

From 10:50 to 11:00, Gabriel's eyes constantly wandered to the main door, his heart quickening at the promise of Valerie Vaughan's arrival. When the clock on his computer read 11:02, he saw her on the other side of the door's glass, swiping her pass card.

He held off on taking another call until she entered and began heading his way.

Valerie Vaughan, the girl he hardly knew and wanted to know everything about.

Ever since his first day on the calling floor, she had caught his eye, and not just because she was beautiful. He had been assigned to his cubicle and when he'd come over and plopped the stack of training manuals down, he'd found his hands and fingers tingling at the sight of the girl sitting diagonally across from him. And when he

FIRST NIGHT OUT

sat down to get himself organized, he couldn't help looking through the small window of glass that ran through the chest-high partitions separating the stations. He didn't know what stole him away first: her soft skin or the rich dark brown hair that ended at her shoulders with tiny ringlets at its end. And though he said hi, all he got in return was a smile before she busied herself with another call.

His affection for her . . . it wasn't just because she was the most gorgeous girl working at Dolla-card. He had been raised well enough to feel uncomfortable to merely look at women and base any thoughts or feelings about them solely on looks. His father had made that much clear throughout the years. But with Valerie, there was just something about her, something *underneath* the girl he saw every day that drew him to her. He just wished he knew what that was and could get to know that part about her better.

This morning, as Valerie, coffee cup in hand, threw her black purse on her desk, Gabriel couldn't help but stare. She glanced his way and brushed a few of those beautiful dark strands away from her brown eyes.

"Good morning," he said.

She didn't reply.

He considered saying it again but with the way she quickly busied herself at her desk, he figured she was probably ignoring him.

If only she'd give him a moment, just a few seconds for general pleasantries, but with Valerie, those were hard to come by. She kept to herself and only talked business with those she worked with. If Gabriel overheard her talking about something not work-related, her tone was always distant and matter-of-fact, as if socializing with people at work was some kind of crime. He just wished he knew why.

Someone came up behind him. "You bored or what?"

Gabriel turned in his seat to see his boss, Rod Hunter, looming over him. *Great.* As much as he liked Rod, he disliked him all the same. The guy wasn't terribly tall, maybe five-eight, five-nine, thick but not muscular, with black hair and brown eyes. The main problem was the guy's attitude and the evident power-tripping he enjoyed in his position as call floor supervisor. Rod had been on the phones, too, at one time. Gabriel knew that because every time he had a problem that required his supervisor's help, Rod would always bring up some call he once took as a rep and use it as an example as to how to resolve the issue; he always seemed to rub it in how much better he was at the job than Gabriel. Gabriel's mental retort was always, *Well, thanks, but I, unlike you, won't be stuck here forever. This is just an in-the-meantime thing for me.*

"No," Gabriel said. "Not bored. Still feeling kinda poor, is all."

Rod crossed his arms. "Yeah, I got your messages. You'll make it through the day though, right?"

Gabriel nodded. "Yeah, but might need a breather here or there."

Rod unfolded his arms and gave Gabriel a pat on the back as he walked past. "Fine, just don't stall too long between calls. Got a queue to keep down."

Gabriel glanced at Valerie.

If only you kn— "What if I showed her?" He mouthed the words silently and was tempted to say them a second time loud and clear. Then the thought went away. But, man, what an opportunity to finally get a real conversation going with her. To tell her about what he could now do, to *show* her, take her hand and lead her into

FIRST NIGHT OUT

the sky—She'd probably fall in love with him. Who wouldn't?

It almost seemed like a good idea, but what if it backfired? His secret would be out and, if Valerie talked, everyone would know and it would lead to a zillion different other problems.

It was almost time for lunch.

Gabriel did his best to focus on his work and took another call, but while he was assisting a customer who didn't seem to understand that shouting was unnecessary, his mind kept drifting over to Valerie.

"Stupid thing," Rod said loudly enough a few aisles over that nearly everyone on the calling floor heard him.

Gabriel, still full from lunch, stood from his seat and glanced over.

Rod banged the side of the black filing cabinet with the palm of his hand; a loud, echoey *boom* rang in the air. A few folks jumped in their seats. He bent down, checked something out of Gabriel's line of sight, then stood, the expression on his face conveying he knew everyone was staring at him. He played it off as if he didn't care. Gripping either side of the four-foot-tall filing cabinet, Rod took a deep breath then began waddling it back down the aisle.

A monotone beep dinged in Gabriel's ear, signaling another call. He didn't answer it but instead imagined himself going over to where Rod was struggling, modestly picking the cabinet up and balancing it on his hand as if it were an empty wastebasket. Valerie would look his way with wide-eyed astonishment as he gingerly walked to the end of the aisle, placed the cabinet down, then casually walked back to his desk as if he'd done nothing out of the ordinary.

Bong. The customer was waiting.

I could so do that, Gabriel thought and sat down. He reached up to his headset, about to remove it. This could be the chance to get Valerie's attention.

Rod grumbled something, but Gabriel couldn't make it out.

Bong.

Brow furrowed, Gabriel pulled his headset off his ears then paused. He didn't know what stopped him. Maybe it was simply not knowing what he'd do precisely after he returned to his seat after an awesome display of strength. Or maybe it was the uncertainty of whether or not Valerie would be impressed with him. He placed the earphones back over his ears and adjusted the headset so it sat squarely on his head.

Bong.

"Okay, okay," he breathed.

The temptation to reveal himself abated a bit. *Just got to make it through the day.* His mind fastforwarded to getting off work no differently than any other day. To go the whole day without letting on things were different would be an accomplishment in itself. His whole life he had always had the bad habit of speaking too soon and acting presumptuously. Often, such rash actions—though not necessarily uncalled for or even harsh—eventually landed him in heaps of trouble, which was why, he suspected, he wasn't as highly thought of as he wished. Why he was never the guy folks looked up to or even took seriously.

I hate being me every day. To make it through today as if things were business-as-usual—it would be a step in the right direction. *What* direction, he didn't know. But if he pulled through and just remained patient, he'd have something that was his. Really his. Something that no one could take away.

Bong.

With a flick of the finger on the LINE button, Gabriel answered the call.

Valerie ignored him the whole afternoon.

Before catching the bus, Gabriel stopped by the newspaper dispensers out front, verifying that his activities the night before had gone unnoticed. The papers, both the *Free Press* and the *Sun,* didn't report anything. He reminded himself that if someone had seen him, it would be page one news and not some story hidden near the classifieds.

As he rode the bus, he imagined himself flying home instead, soaring high above the city streets and making it back to his apartment in no time.

I can't keep doing this, he thought, *keep keeping it in.* His heart ached. *And it's only been one day. To go through any more . . .*

When he got home, he felt as if he'd just done something wrong. Guilt mixed with a heart-stirring longing filled him. It was more feeling than thought and as much as he tried to pinpoint what was bothering him, he couldn't.

Early evening sunlight cast his place in a yellowy glow. Too bright, especially for the gloom raging within.

Gabriel removed his shoes, drew the blinds and sat on the couch.

He remained there till dark, ignoring the phone every time it rang, ignoring his stomach every time it growled for something to eat.

"I can't keep this to myself," he said. *Should I have done something? Acted in some way?*

He let his mind drift. Valerie had ignored him till it was time for him to leave. It was as if he didn't exist. Just some guy she worked with who didn't matter. Either she was extraordinarily stuck up or had made it her business to not get involved with anyone at work. She surely would have looked his way if he had done what he had thought of doing: taking her by the hand and leading her into the sky.

"But for something like this," he said, "it can't be all about me." The messenger said it was a gift, and gifts were something one used wisely. What was he expected to do? All his life he had been just Gabriel Garrison, nobody-at-large.

More than anything he wanted to be noticed, if for no other reason than to prove to himself he wasn't worthless.

"But I must be special . . . at least in some small way, right?" he whispered. "The messenger wouldn't have chosen me for no reason." The idea made him feel a little better. "To go out there and pronounce myself, what, all-powerful—I don't think that would work. Sure, you'd be deemed incredible but everyone would be at your side twenty-four-seven." *Look at movie stars. They can't go anywhere without cameras constantly hovering around them and people wanting autographs. I'm sure it's all fine and good for a while but it must get tiring.*

Then an idea hit him. "That's ridiculous," he said. "Isn't it?"

CHAPTER SEVEN

GETTING THROUGH WORK the next day wasn't any easier. If anything, it was a lot worse. For Gabriel to just sit there in his cubicle and plow through call after call and pretend his mind wasn't racing with thoughts and scenarios involving his powers—He wasn't sure how much more he could take.

A part of him was able to suppress the strong desire to fly to and from work, to bite his tongue and not tell Valerie this latest news about himself, to not just walk out of work after a tough call, never to return, only to later use his powers for some kind of income. Yet another part—a stronger part—yearned to break free, to stand and point the finger at himself and shout, "Here I am! Look at me! Look what I can do! See, I do have something going for me!"

The only thing that kept him level was a secret promise to himself: if he exercised self-control, if he held his powers in check and kept them to himself, then he'd be able to come away with an accomplishment he doubted many could actually do. He lived in a world where self-centeredness and the rat race dominated everything. To go up against the world, to actually take a stand and say, "Wait. I'm better than this. What I have here is remarkable, but I'm not going to squander it because I don't have any patience and all I want is glory," that would set him apart from the rest and make him special in some small way.

When 4:00 rolled around and it was time to go, Gabriel left the office satisfied that he hadn't given in. And when he boarded the bus just like everybody else instead of finding an alleyway he could fly off from, he actually felt like a person of worth, someone who wasn't an accident or just one of several billion faces that didn't matter in the grand scheme of things. For an instant, he had pride.

The bus wasn't too crowded. He found a seat near the back, crossed his arms and gazed out the window. The bus got moving and those on the sidewalks faded from view. He shifted his gaze to a copy of the *Winnipeg Free Press* that lay on the seat beside him. He picked it up and flipped through it, anything to take his mind off the constant torrent of superpowered thoughts. None of the stories in the first few pages caught his interest. Until he reached page four, where there was an article about a little girl who was killed when gang members entered her father's house, demanding money for drugs. The father was half-dead when police found him after finally arriving on the scene two hours later. He died six hours afterward in the hospital. One of the neighbors, the article said, saw the group of four or five youths break in, but didn't say anything to them or call the police for fear of getting involved. The neighbor had only come forward now because police were questioning people in the area and he wanted a clean conscience.

Scrunching up the paper in his hand, Gabriel's heart sped, hurting and angry. *No one said anything,* he thought. *No one* did *anything.*

Suddenly everything became clear.

FIRST NIGHT OUT

The second he got in the door at home, he went to the kitchen, pulled out a notepad and pen and began drawing. The night before he had wondered if he could somehow disguise himself so as to not attract too much attention, but that was as far as the thought got. The idea of doing anything helpful as "himself" seemed somehow . . . out there. If people suddenly knew what he could do they'd be all over him, getting him to do things he didn't want to do and never give any him peace about it. What he'd do after he disguised himself, he hadn't a clue.

Until now.

Could it work? he wondered. *That girl* . . . "No one helped her. She probably couldn't even speak up for herself even if she wanted to."

His heart panged at the thought of a young wide-eyed girl frozen in terror as gang members raided her father's house, her little mind unable to comprehend why these strangers wanted to hurt her daddy. The article implied she was killed first, but there was a good chance she had witnessed the youths beat and torment her father before they ended her life. Gabriel could only imagine the fear and panic that overtook her and how any shred of sanity must have been robbed when she saw her father, the one person in all the world whom she thought could stand up to anything, get thrown around and beaten black and blue. Gabriel put himself behind her eyes and imagined his own father being beaten. He could only hold the thought for a moment before he felt the tears begin to rise.

"I know what it's like not to be heard," he whispered. "To go unnoticed and not be taken seriously. I know I'm not alone in that, but it still feels like it." Another sharp pang stung his heart. "I may not be the most special person in all the world, but if I'm able to do something, to help others feel of worth and somehow protect them from those who would bring them down" —he paused and swallowed the dry lump in his throat— "then I'll do it." He exhaled slowly. *And maybe then I'll feel like somebody who is worthwhile, too, even if it's only for a moment.*

He adjusted the notepad before him so it was centered. An interesting figure looked back, one of crude dark lines and light blue shading.

"Something like that," he said, sniffling. He wiped his eyes. "Just needs a bit of work."

———

It had taken a few hours to get the design just right. When he felt it was finished, Gabriel held the notepad an arms length from his face and studied it.

"Yeah, I like that," he said softly.

He went to the couch in the front room, kitchen light still on, and fell asleep.

All through the next day at work, he kept thinking about his drawing and what his next step was. Even Valerie wasn't much of a distraction when she came in mid morning. Though he looked at her every now and then, his mind was too preoccupied with what was to come to even think about her not giving him any attention.

His drawing . . .

If she only knew . . . he thought more than once. *But she'd probably think I'm crazy for doing it.*

When he got home, he had a grilled cheese sandwich and a glass of juice, then went to the bedroom and dug the notepad out of the bottom of his underwear drawer.

Notepad in hand, he retreated to the linen closet and pulled out his mother's old sewing kit and machine down from the top shelf. He never understood why she had given it to him other than her stating he might need it one day. Now, he was thankful she had. He went to the living room and got to work on the real life construction of the image on the pad's front page.

Having taken Home-Ec in junior high was a big help, though it was never his strong suit. Most of what he learned he had forgotten, but the basics of sewing still remained.

I guess they do teach you that stuff for a reason after all, he mused.

He pulled out the tape measure and stripped down to his boxers and took his measurements. After jotting the info down, he booted up his computer and hit the Internet, seeking guidance. The next step would be to come up with a pattern for the outfit he designed. It took a few visits to different websites to find the right how-to articles, but he managed to download enough information to get the project underway.

After printing the pages, he set them aside and took the stack of blank paper from beside the printer and got to the task of taping the sheets together, some long and narrow, others big and wide. Soon his floor was covered in white, with blue markings in pen as to what each sheet was for in the top right corners.

Using the pages he printed out and the design on his notepad as a guide, Gabriel got to work.

It took three long evenings to draw out the various shapes he'd need to construct the bodysuit, chest piece, gloves, boots, belt and mask. The cape, as straight forward as he thought it should have been, was the toughest. It wasn't just an issue of having a huge piece of fabric to wrap around yourself. Making it part of the chest piece took the most time and getting the inches precise took even longer. He thought of scrapping the cape idea, but without it, he knew he'd feel stupid. The cape not only acted as a shield to cover what he was really wearing, but it also carried a regal bearing to it, a majestic quality that looked good on paper. He hoped it would look just as good in real life. To just run around in tights . . .

"I *am* going to wear tights, aren't I?" he said. And saying it out loud seemed to hammer home the point. *Why tights? What was I thinking? Maybe I should just toss this and start over? Just wear normal clothes or something.* But he knew he couldn't. If he went out wearing merely jeans and a sweatshirt and a toque with eyeholes cut out, it wouldn't be the same. He had to stand out, to become something *different*. Everyday people blended into one another. To inspire, to stir hearts, he had to become a beacon of some kind and just wearing a sweatshirt and jeans wouldn't cut it.

Just make it and see how you look, he thought and proceeded with the finishing touches to the patterns before cutting them out.

The next day after coming home from work, he made a night out of bussing around to three different fabric stores (to avoid suspicion if he actually went through with this), purchasing the lengths of material and thread he needed and a little bit extra in case he screwed up. When he took a huge roll of light blue material to the counter, the clerk asked him what he was working on.

"A blanket for my mom," he said. He paid the bill and as he exited the store, he realized what he'd just done. *Am I going to have to be dishonest with everybody?* To do that made him what he was trying not to be. It didn't sit right. He resolved to tell the truth as much as possible from then on, knowing that once he started down a path of a little lies, the next thing he'd know he wouldn't know fact from fiction and would probably end up weaving a web of deceit so thick he'd never find his way out.

Over the next two days, Gabriel cut the fabric according to the patterns. Once done, he surveyed the heap of cloth. It didn't look like much, just a mountain of material that could have been anything.

"Give it time," he said.

He finished the night pinning the various pieces in all the right places, getting them ready for sewing tomorrow.

When that time came, he set his sewing machine up on the kitchen table and stared at it. He couldn't remember how to thread the needle and it took a few tries till he thought he had it right. He even went to the Internet to see if someone knew how to thread his particular machine. No one did, but he made do. He reached for the pieces of pinned material that would become the forearms to his gloves—something simple, just a straight sewing line—then stopped himself when he recalled his Home-Ec's teachers words of caution: "Always test your needle first." He set the forearm pieces down and folded a scrap piece of fabric in half then ran the edges through the machine. He had forgotten how hard the machine grabbed the material and how quickly it rushed it through. He had to adjust his foot on the pedal to get the speed down to a moderate pace. Once the fabric went through, Gabriel snipped the thread on one of its ends, freeing it from the machine. He studied it. The thread fastened the edges together in a small and tight line.

"Not bad for a guy who hasn't done this in years," he said.

He practiced on a few more pieces before attempting the forearm pieces of his glove.

"Go slow," he said as he pushed the pieces through. When the thread line was complete, he clipped the end and examined his work. It was perfect. "Say that when you're doing the mask, then we'll talk," he added with a grin.

The night wore on and so did the next and so did the next, each hour put in one step closer to breathing life into something that was a mere two-dimensional image on a piece of paper.

As each portion of the costume was completed, he tried it on, making sure it fit. A couple of times the seam had been a little off, in turn making bending an elbow or knee difficult. And each time, he had to carefully take out the thread and start over. But with each pass through the machine, he found himself getting more and more comfortable putting the suit together.

———

It had been over a week since he'd first settled on the design and he had yet to put everything on as a complete outfit. All that was left was running a tight and thick elastic through the top of the mask and sealing it in, and he'd be done. Finding an appropriate length was the hardest. It took countless trips to the hallway mirror and countless tries to find a length of elastic that would hold the mask to his face but not leave a dark red band on his forehead.

Once everything was pinned in place, he ran the mask through the machine, slow and careful because he was sewing inside a circle. He had learned how difficult "circular sewing" was when sewing thin rubber soles into the tight boots and had nearly lost the whole leg of the bodysuit.

FIRST NIGHT OUT

When the elastic headband was sewn in, Gabriel carefully tied the thread in a tight knot, sealing his line, then clipped the split ends as close to the knot as possible.

This better not look stupid, he thought.

The mask was a part of the bodysuit, so the only way to test what he had created would be to put the whole thing on and look in the mirror.

"Well, might as well put on everything and see how it looks," he said as he pushed himself away from the table.

He took the remaining bits of costume from around the sewing machine, draped them over his arms, turned the machine off, and brought the portions of costume to their counterparts lying on his bed.

He began to get dressed.

As he pulled the suit on over his legs and slid his arms into the sleeves, something was happening within. It was as though he weren't just merely putting on a costume, but a tangible piece of the hope and confidence he was trying to become and attain. With each little pull and twist on the fabric as he fit it into place, more and more he forgot what he was doing and instead began losing himself in the moment.

Once the bodysuit was on, he consciously avoided checking himself in the bedroom mirror, deciding to wait till everything was on first. He scooped the chest piece and cape off the bed, dug around underneath it for the arm and head holes and sat it in place. He fastened the light blue tougher material that ran diagonally across his chest and back to his shoulders and smoothed out the Velcro that kept the light blue piece in place on the bodysuit. The cape wasn't as heavy as he had expected, and this was without his powers activated. He tucked the thin-fabric backpack under his cape and pulled it over his shoulders. Clasping the belt buckle shut cinched up the waistline and drew in the last remainder of poofy light blue from the chest piece.

After he slipped on the gloves, he reached for the mask that was bundled up around his throat like a turtle neck.

He paused before pulling it up and took a deep breath.

"Now or never," he said and tugged the mask up into place. *Now let's see how this looks.*

Gabriel stepped in front of his bedroom mirror, clad in his new outfit. The light blue cape, which blended into the chest piece, sat regally on his shoulders. His power ignited; his blue-sheened hair mixed nicely with the light and dark blue of his mask. The form-fitting bodysuit snugged up against his frame beautifully. He hadn't realized how well defined he was until now. If he didn't know any better, he wouldn't know he was looking at himself.

Perfect.

"You can do this," he told himself. "It's okay if you feel a little silly. But the good you'll do . . ."

While he had constructed the costume, he gave further thought as to *why* he was going to do this. True, a part of it was to make him feel better about himself, to give himself a sense of self-worth, but as he sewed, he understood it was more than that.

It wasn't only about him.

It was about people.

It was about upholding what was right. About restoring hope. And though he was only one man, history had shown that even one man could make a difference.

It was about promoting an ideal and taking a stand for what was right and true.

FIRST NIGHT OUT

He'd be an axiom man to the city. Something they could look up to, an example they could follow. An ideal of truth. Though it was possible he was putting himself up on a pedestal by doing so, he also knew—even about himself—that people needed to see something larger than life to get them to look to the sky for hope.

Ready, he went to his balcony, peeked out the window to make sure no one was watching, and when he was confident no one was, he stepped outside.

Embracing the air never felt so good.

Okay, make the mental shift. You're "Axiom-man" *now. Not Gabriel Garrison,* he thought. *"Axiom-man," huh? That'll take some getting used to.*

A flush of heat rushed over him and suddenly he felt like an idiot. Kids ran around in costumes and pretended to play hero. Not grown men. Whatever feelings he had about this being a good idea quickly abated.

He thought back to what he looked like in his bedroom mirror and though the image before him had been one of, well, a hero, something about all this still didn't feel right. Despite what he could do, regardless that even now he was flying through the air, something which gave him license to wear tights and a cape, he still felt ridiculous.

"I can't show anybody this," he said. He glanced down at himself as he flew along. Dark blue, tight-clad legs were tucked up beneath him; a light blue cape flapped against his ankles. "Oh, man, who am I kidding?"

Axiom-man wanted to turn around and go home. If no one saw him tonight, it'd be like this whole thing never happened and he could think of something else to do with his powers.

No, he thought. *Just ride it out. You're just having a knee-jerk reaction to all this. It'll pass.* But he wasn't sure it would.

And there was something that scared him even more.

Chapter Eight

Heart racing, anxiety coating his stomach like a foul flu, Axiom-man stayed high above the city streets, far enough away from the tops of the buildings that if anyone glanced up into the night sky, they wouldn't see him. But at some point, he'd have to go lower if he was going to follow through on what he had set out to do. Whatever sense of comfort and relief he had felt about heading out to help people had disappeared. All that remained was the desire to help.

"But desire to act and actually acting are two different things," he muttered.

He had never been one for confrontation. Most times, when someone rubbed him the wrong way or raised a fuss about an issue, he retreated into himself and took whatever was thrown at him on the chin. And that was the exact opposite of the type of attitude he'd need if he were to be of any help to anybody.

Man, I hope nothing happens, he thought. At least that way, he could still come home with the subtle satisfaction that, despite no one seeing him, he had still "gone out there." Still made the effort. *But not every night is going to be like that even if that's how tonight pans out.*

At some point he'd have to interact, and when that time came, it would lock him into a way of life he wasn't sure he was ready for. A person dressed like him, someone making their intentions blatantly clear, couldn't just show up one day, help another soul, then disappear, never to be seen or heard from again. And most certainly he couldn't allow himself to help out once, take some time off, then come back to it weeks, months or even years later.

There would be no turning back once he made himself known.

If I could just pop in, help somebody, then take off back into the shadows or into the sky, then maybe this wouldn't be too bad. He nodded to himself. "Yeah, that's what I'll do."

He read stories in the paper now and then, those about heroes, everyday folk lending someone else a hand in a big way, then disappearing without concern for credit in the papers. He supposed his costume acted in the same way. He hadn't even recognized himself when he looked in the mirror earlier. Certainly no one else would, especially since those who knew Gabriel Garrison were limited to only family, a few friends and some of his coworkers.

For a while there, he had forgotten he *was* wearing a costume, an outfit people were supposed to have grown out of after their last teenage Halloween outing.

Nobody better see me, he thought adamantly.

Taking a deep breath, he doubled back through the air and flew downward. The city streets grew closer and he hoped that his costume was dark enough to blend in with the shadows of the night and, in combination with the glare from the streetlights, keep him invisible.

Just fly fast. Even if someone saw you, it'd probably take them a minute to process what *they saw and they'd probably dismiss it as their eyes playing tricks on them. People don't fly. And they don't run around in tights either.*

FIRST NIGHT OUT

He kept himself about thirty feet above the rooftops along Portage Avenue, then went about flying up and down each street, not really sure what he was looking for or what he was doing.

A patrol, he supposed. Cops did it all the time and responded when needed.

I'm on patrol, he thought, the notion alien to him. When walking about the streets himself, he nine times out of ten had an agenda and it was always an issue of just going from Point A to Point B. Now, playing the whatever-I-find-I-find hand was very foreign.

Heart still beating rapidly, he hoped that nothing would require his assistance.

Axiom-man spent the night going up and down the streets, now and then soaring a few thousand feet into the sky for a breather. As the hours passed, he got more and more used to wearing the costume.

"Hmph, maybe for now, but ask me if I'm comfortable when I have to actually show myself to somebody."

One of the outdoor clocks read 12:42. Another hour and he'd head on home.

Axiom-man flew over the Exchange District not far from his day job.

A siren blared up and his heart slammed into his ribcage. He surveyed the street below and a cop car flashed its lights and sounded its siren and crossed through a red light. On the other side of the intersection, it turned its siren off and drove along, everything seeming all right.

I hate it when they do that, he thought.

He banked left and flew over a couple of alleys.

A scream sounded from below.

A.P. FUCHS

It took Axiom-man about a minute to locate the source of the scream. He landed on a rooftop overlooking a poorly lit alley.

"Somebody HEEEELPP!" The woman's voice went raw on the last word as she ran down the back lane. "Heeelp, plee-ee-ee-ease." Sobs laced her voice; she wiped the tears from her eyes as she ran.

Two men ran after her, one tall and bulky, the other about the same height but noticeably slimmer. They both wore jean jackets.

"Hey, get back here!" one of them said, his shout low and scratchy.

The woman's heels rapidly clacked against the pavement as she tried to outrun her pursuers. The purse strap over her shoulder kept sliding down into the crook of her elbow and each time she reached across with her other hand to push it back up, her run slowed.

The men burst into a full sprint.

There wasn't much time.

Axiom-man crept as close to the edge as possible and got a better look. *Don't just stay here. You have to do something.* But try as he might to move, he remained planted.

Below, the clacking of the woman's heels increased in intensity until—*Kaclik!* She tumbled forward so fast she didn't have time to put her hands out before her. She hit the pavement with a sickening thud and lay there face down, not moving. The men caught up to her, each taking an arm, and hoisted her to her feet. Only when she was standing did she seem to realize the danger she was in and started kicking and screaming as the men dragged her further back into the alley, out of sight from the street.

The men threw her up against the wall.

FIRST NIGHT OUT

Axiom-man was appalled that no one had yet come to the rescue. You could hear the woman's cries and pleas for help a mile away.

Get moving, he told himself. His heart beat so fast and hard that he felt its resounding thumps in every inch of his body. Sudden heat flushed over him and his skin went damp. *You have to do something. Calm down.* But his thudding heart refused to obey. No matter. He had to press on.

As he edged along the rooftop over the group of three below, he knew he had all of two seconds to make a decision if he was going to get involved or not. Those seconds moved by slow, as if minutes, and a million questions raced through his mind. Would he have to fight these men? Probably. Would they fight back? More than likely. And he was afraid what he might end up doing to them if he had to defend himself. He hadn't tested his superpowered strength combat-wise and the closest he'd gotten to doing so was when he'd smashed those wooden beams on the train. The beams had blown into splinters with each strike. To do that to someone else's head . . . . And if or when these guys fought back, he didn't know if he could take them both. He'd never been in a fight before and had no idea how he would fare. But with his superstrength, he could most likely take them down. Still, if one got a good, clean shot in, it could be all over. He had to keep his distance, if possible. And though these worries were understandable—it was his first night out, after all—he also realized they had no place with him tonight nor any other night he'd don the cape.

"No, no, please, I beg you. Stop!" the woman said below.

"Too bad," the bigger man said and yanked her purse off her arm.

81

When she reached forward to get it back, the slimmer man socked her one across the cheekbone. The woman crumpled to the ground, knees up, face in her hands, wailing.

That's it, Axiom-man thought, grimacing beneath his mask.

He shook apprehensively at what he was about to do, but also couldn't help but smile at the prospect of putting an end to this madness.

Okay, get in, get out and you're done.

Taking a deep breath, he dove off the rooftop and soared quietly into the sky, high enough that the men below wouldn't see him. Holding his cape to his body so it wouldn't flap in the wind on the way down, he gently landed behind the two men, about six feet away.

This was it.

No turning back.

What do I say? But the words came, his voice low and firm. "Gentlemen."

The two men whirled around, their eyes wild with reckless hate yet wide enough to convey a sense of fear at being caught.

"Give the purse back," he said.

The two men looked at each other, their dark bangs swaying across their foreheads as they moved their necks. Both cracked up laughing.

The thought came out of nowhere, but Axiom-man couldn't help but think it: *I knew it. I look stupid.*

"Oh, man, I can't believe this," the slimmer guy said, pointing at Axiom-man.

The big guy nodded. "Very nice."

Ignore them. The sooner you get this over with, the sooner everyone goes home. "I said, 'Give the purse back.'"

FIRST NIGHT OUT

The woman pulled her face from her hands and looked up at him, her cheeks stained with tears, her lip and nose bloody. Her long black hair hid the rest of her face, but her piercing blue eyes were wide with fear.

"And I suppose you're gonna make me?" Slim said.

Axiom-man didn't know what to say and he suddenly felt foolish. The circumstance seemed . . . smaller . . . somehow, and his first thought was that they could talk this out and shake hands in the end. "Give. The purse. Back," he repeated.

The bigger guy walked up to him slow and sure, bobbing his head from side to side, checking him out.

Axiom-man's heart jumped inside when the man stepped within an arm's reach.

Big Guy turned and faced his comrade, and this time it was his buddy's turn to point. With a squealy laugh, he said, "This is too funny." And he rejoined his friend.

"Please, help me," the woman said, her voice a tear-soaked whisper.

Nervous as anything, Axiom-man nodded to her. He spoke as slowly and firmly as he could muster. "I'm only going to ask once more. Give the purse back and walk away."

The two men looked at each other again.

"Come and get it," Slim said and brought the purse eyelevel, showing it off.

"You don't want to make me do that," Axiom-man said. The grimace returned and he was growing tired with the lack of progress. These guys thought he was just a nut in a Halloween costume. They had no idea what he was capable of. His panicking heart suddenly thrilled at the thought of scaring these guys with a powerful display. But he'd only play that card if he needed to. *Play their game, but*

83

if they try and take you out—Bring them down! Then in afterthought, *Just be careful doing so.*

Axiom-man, ready for one or both of them to pounce on him any second, slowly stepped toward Slim and when he was close enough, grabbed the purse as fast as he could and ripped it away.

Slim's eyes went wide; he clearly didn't expect the purse to be taken so easily.

The moment Axiom-man had the purse in hand, Big Guy growled and reached for him, and wrapped his thick arms around him, going immediately for Axiom-man's mask. He tried to tear it off. Slim moved in right after and yanked the purse from Axiom-man's hands.

Putting the purse out of his mind for a moment, Axiom-man reached up to where Big Guy clawed at his face and forcefully dug his fingers in between Big Guy's hand and his face and pulled the man's hand away. Axiom-man squeezed the man's hand until he felt bones crushing beneath the skin. Big Guy howled and cursed and took a step back. Axiom-man whirled around and delivered a swift left wallop to the side of Big Guy's head. The man dropped as if someone had grabbed him by the collar of his jean jacket and yanked him to the ground.

Eyes blazing blue energy, Axiom-man turned to face Slim, but already Slim was running down the alley. Before he took off to follow him, Axiom-man glanced toward the woman. She recoiled, drawing her legs up tight against herself, trying to hug the wall like a child clasping for dear life to its parent's leg.

*She thinks I'm going to—*He fixed his gaze on Slim.

Curling his fingers into his palms, he raised his fists and arms and left the ground. Letting the moment take him, the thrill of the hunt and the joy of the chase, Axiom-man soared through the air and quickly caught up to Slim. He flew over the man's head and landed on the other side. Slim stopped his sprint and staggered back a couple of steps.

"No, you didn't just—" he stammered.

"Yes, I did," Axiom-man said, closing the distance between them. He snuffed out the blue energy in his eyes.

Slim took a swing. His fist came in fast and Axiom-man took the blow in his shoulder, sending a numb tingle down his arm. Rolling his shoulder, shaking it off, Axiom-man grabbed Slim's collar with his left hand and brought the man swiftly to the right, then with a hard yank, jerked him to the left, tossing him up against the alley's brick wall. Slim hit the brick with a smack then fell to the ground where he immediately clasped both hands behind his head, rolling in pain.

In his peripheral, Axiom-man caught a glimpse of the woman some thirty feet away. She was standing now, body slightly leaning to the side as she peered down the alley to see what was happening toward its mouth.

"No, no, don't," Slim said.

Resolving not to say anything further to this guy, Axiom-man grabbed him, snapped him upward and pushed him up against the wall. Slim's eyes rolled back in their sockets and Axiom-man thought the guy might have a concussion. When Slim focused, Axiom-man ignited the blue energy in his eyes and stared into the man's brown-eyed gaze.

Slim socked Axiom-man in the nose, and when his vision blurred then cleared a moment later, he saw the sense of fear in Slim's eyes, as if the fellow couldn't believe he had just taken another shot at him.

Axiom-man adjusted his grip on Slim's jacket, then hauled him up into the air and flew him over to where his buddy lay on the ground. With a hard downswing, he hurled Slim's body from ten feet up onto Big Guy's back. When Slim hit, his body shook once, then didn't move at all.

The woman yelped and covered her mouth.

Axiom-man touched down and was surprised to see Slim still holding the purse in his fingers. He bent down, pulled it away, then offered it to the woman.

She just stood there, afraid to take it.

"It's all right," he said.

Her eyes never left his. He realized his were still crackling with blue energy. He powered them down.

When she still didn't come any closer, he walked up to her and quickened his pace when she began to move away.

"I'm not going to hurt you," he said and offered her the purse again.

She remained still for a moment, then with a shaky hand, reached for her purse. He made sure she held it firmly in her fingers before he let go.

The two gazed at each for several seconds before Axiom-man glanced back at the two men lying in a heap.

When he faced her again, she was staring at them, too. A moment later her eyes met his. She didn't need to say anything. Her subtle smile said it all and bathed her bloody face with a warm glow.

Axiom-man brought his index finger to his nose. "Shhh."

He took a step back and reached upward. He didn't have to look back down after his feet left the ground to know she was staring after him.

Epilogue

As Axiom-Man soared through the sky, a calmness came over his heart as he replayed the event over in his mind. It was that woman's smile that brought a sense of comfort to his unease and rid his body of the adrenaline coursing through it.

He had made a difference.

The woman was okay. Those men tasted justice.

And, after years of struggling with self-worth, constantly thinking he never measured up, for the first time, he was at peace with himself.

Embracing the air never felt so good.

ABOUT THE AUTHOR

A.P. Fuchs is the author of several novels and writes from Winnipeg, Manitoba. Among his most recent are *Doorway of Darkness*, *Axiom-man*, *The Way of the Fog*, and *April*, which was written under the pseudonym, Peter Fox. Visit his corner of the Web at **www.apfuchs.com**

Printed in the United States
84017LV00001B/217-315/A